"Emma, turn towa

Rafe demanded, not ca
"Tilt your head down, eyes up at me."

Without a word, Emma did, and he took those shots, too. Her slight stiffness actually worked in his favor, the slightly shy, outrageously sexy schoolgirl. It was wrong but he wanted her, wanted so damn much. By the time he put down the camera, his hands were shaking.

"Is that it?" she asked, still leaning against the lockers.

"That's it."

She pushed away and walked toward him, every sway of her hips a slam to his gut.

"What are you doing?" he asked, and backed up a step.

She didn't stop until their toes touched. "I didn't like that."

"I didn't, either."

She cocked a hip and looked at him from carefully made-up eyes. "And I don't like you."

He waited, tense, for what she would say next.

"But I've never wanted you more," she said in a frustrated voice.

That was all the invitation he needed....

Blaze™

Dear Reader,

I really wondered whether I had another Blaze story in me. The sexy premises always seem to escape me. Then my husband got this wildly sexy calendar from a friend—twelve shots of beautiful women in erotic poses—and I thought, surely, these women are just like me. Well, except for the perfect bodies and gorgeous faces, that is.

That calendar started me thinking how a woman would find herself posing for such pictures, and *Bared* was born. Take one hot, but slightly repressed soap opera writer and one sexy, but slightly attitudinal photographer stuck together for this job of shooting twelve months of fantasies....

Some of you might recognize my hero Rafe in this story. He briefly appeared in my February 2004 Temptation novel , *Back in the Bedroom*. I hope you enjoy reading his story!

Happy reading,

Jill Shalvis

Books by Jill Shalvis

HARLEQUIN TEMPTATION

804—OUT OF THE BLUE
822—CHANCE ENCOUNTER
845—AFTERSHOCK
861—A PRINCE OF A GUY
878—HER PERFECT STRANGER
885—FOR THE LOVE OF NICK
910—ROUGHING IT WITH RYAN*
914—TANGLING WITH TY*
918—MESSING WITH MAC*
938—LUKE

HARLEQUIN SINGLE TITLE

THE STREET WHERE SHE LIVES

HARLEQUIN DUETS

42—KISS ME, KATIE!
HUG ME, HOLLY!
57—BLIND DATE DISASTERS
EAT YOUR HEART OUT
85—A ROYAL MESS
HER KNIGHT TO REMEMBER

HARLEQUIN BLAZE

63—NAUGHTY BUT NICE

HARLEQUIN FLIPSIDE

5—NATURAL BLOND INSTINCTS

*South Village Singles

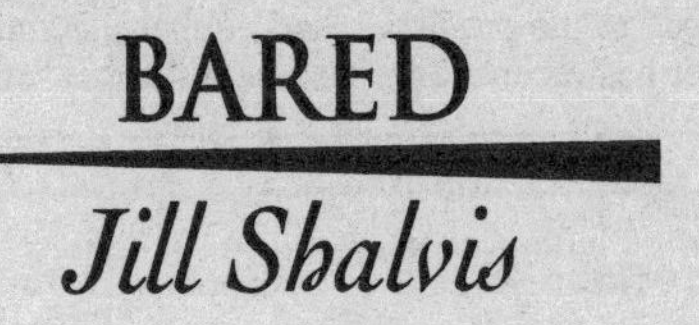

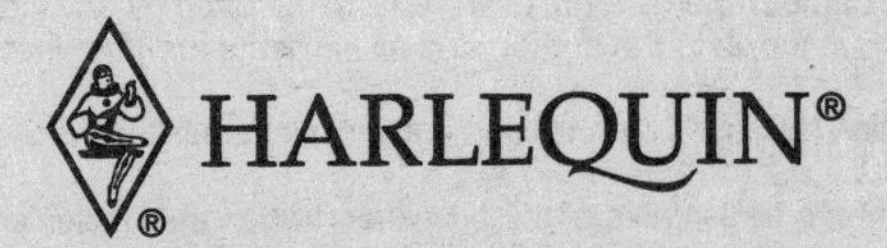

TORONTO • NEW YORK • LONDON
AMSTERDAM • PARIS • SYDNEY • HAMBURG
STOCKHOLM • ATHENS • TOKYO • MILAN • MADRID
PRAGUE • WARSAW • BUDAPEST • AUCKLAND

ISBN 0-373-79136-4

BARED

This edition published by arrangement with Harlequin Books S.A.

www.eHarlequin.com

Printed in U.S.A.

1

RAFE DELACANTRO WAS IN HELL and, as usual, it was a woman's fault.

The lush, vibrant green tropical forest of Kauai surrounded him. With the hanging vines and myriad trees and bushes, not to mention the buzz of strange and exotic insects and who knew what else, the place was a virtual paradise.

But all he felt was pent-up frustration and resentment, both of which he needed to get rid of in order to make this photo shoot work. It was his last photo shoot, at least for Hollywood, and he couldn't wait to get it done. For ten years he'd been snapping images of the rich and famous, the spoiled beauties, the up-and-comers, working mostly in fashion and for magazines, making a name for himself as one of the best photographers. And it had been a good run. He was proud of all that he'd accomplished.

But at age thirty-two he was tired of the demands, of the games. Tired of being at the beck and call of people who had too much fame, too much money and not a clue as to what real life was about.

Rafe had a clue, and he wanted more of it.

Still, being a photographer defined him, so he wouldn't—couldn't—retire his camera entirely. After this last series of shoots, he'd use a camera for himself only, trying his hand at something other than people. Plants, landscapes, even animals—anything that couldn't talk back, argue or con. Yeah, his retirement was well earned and it would be amazing.

As soon as this job was done—this one last favor for a good friend. It was a calendar spread, twelve months of fantasies…which, for Rafe, equaled twelve different, difficult shoots in various locales. They were working on the March page of the calendar today, and his crew stood by. The lighting seemed perfect at the moment, but given the rumbling in the sky, this would be temporary.

They really needed to get started right now, but they were missing one important, necessary element—the model.

Hence his frustration, resentment and seething temper.

Finally, just as the last of his patience vanished, she showed up, taking her sweet time sauntering through the muggy, steamy heat down the path toward the crew as if she had all day. Her eyes—a light amber color that matched her name—were hidden behind mirrored sunglasses. Amber's hair tumbled past her shoulders free and unencumbered, as he'd requested. One thing going his way, at least. Her long, willowy body was covered by a wraparound skirt and a T-shirt, because he happened to be holding her costume in his hand. But he had no doubt that her mouthwatering form, the one that had graced many a B movie and more than her share of dubious-quality Web sites, would be perfect for what he had in mind.

He stood in the middle of the set that, thanks to the incredible beauty of the island, was comprised of a naturally mossy floor, a half circle of bushes and a hammock swinging gently between two trees. A gazebo completed the backdrop. It began to lightly rain and steam rose from everything, an effect that they couldn't have created anywhere but here on the island. Just out of the camera's range were the bulbs, the cords and the blocking required to capture the lighting just right—lighting they were losing as the fog lowered.

"About time," he said, knowing she'd lower her sunglasses and flash him her impetuous grin, not caring about anyone's schedule but her own.

Amber didn't care about much other than herself, a fact he'd learned five minutes into their one and only date a few years back. She had no interest in anything other than her own reflection in a mirror—though she'd been both shocked and infuriated when he hadn't wanted to continue seeing her.

They'd worked together occasionally since that disastrous date when she'd been late, needy, bitchy and pure trouble the entire night. And every single time since, she'd amused herself by messing with him on the sets in various annoying ways, so he expected no less today. But he'd promised Stone, his oldest friend and assistant, that he'd put both their names on this calendar because the studio behind it had promised to set Stone up for many more, launching his career as a photographer. So Rafe had to get past the urge to wrap his fingers around Amber's pretty neck.

It was just too bad that giving Stone a foot in the industry door left Rafe stuck dealing with Amber, as the calendar would feature her likeness in each of the twelve fantasies. They'd already completed two of the months and Amber had been a pain his ass for each—arriving late, griping about the accommodations, wanting special treatment at every turn. Stone figured she wasn't done torturing Rafe for not wanting to go out with her.

Rafe didn't care. All he cared about was getting done. And with the French maid fantasy—January—and the Amazon jungle fantasy—February—both under his belt now, he was on his way.

Two down, ten more to go…

"Thank you for being only an hour late," he said. "We've nearly lost the light I want, so hustle." He tossed her the costume.

She caught it and looked down at the filmy white "virginal" negligee—with her dewy and unbelievably perfect skin, the images would be sexy, erotic. "What's this?"

"Your costume. Go change."

Amber held the two-piece outfit between long fingers. The bottoms were a couple of strips of white satin. The top had more material but in this case, "more" was relative. Basically she held a gauzy length of fabric that would be draped around her as she lounged on the hammock in that glorious Kauai setting.

As she stared at the costume, a few more raindrops started to fall. Big, fat ones. Damn it, he was not going to stay another day in paradise; he had his own paradise to get back to, his new house in the hills above L.A. "Hurry, Amber."

She looked at the sky. "The weather—"

"Yeah, but if you hurry, we might get this done before suffering electrocution by lightning." He put his hands on her shoulders and turned her around, nudging her toward the makeshift change room—really nothing more than a few bamboo poles and some sheets—off to the side of the set. He watched her move woodenly toward it and narrowed his eyes.

Please don't have a tantrum, he thought, *not today, not now.* But something was off with her. She wasn't giving him and everyone else around her usual I'm-so-hot-look-at-me strut. She wasn't asking for anything special or calling for assistance.

If she was high, he'd have to kill her. No one did drugs on his shoots. "What's the matter with you?"

She went still for one telling moment. "Nothing."

He glanced over at Stone. Also accustomed to Amber's usual antics, his friend just shook his head and lifted a shoulder. He was clueless, as well.

Then Amber turned back toward him, still dangling her outfit from her fingers as if it were day-old trash, which made no sense because she loved to show off her body and nothing would show it off more than that outfit.

A distant boom of thunder made her jump as if she'd never heard thunder before. ''I think maybe we should cancel,'' she said.

She didn't want to show off her gorgeous figure to everyone within a five-mile radius? She didn't want to preen, making everyone on the set drool with lust?

Why?

He racked his brain for reasons, the obvious being that he'd made her mad recently. But he'd done nothing that he could think of, except maybe when he'd refused to escort her to that party she'd wanted to go to after their last shoot in Hollywood.

Parties didn't interest him any more than a night with Amber did. He didn't want to hang around women in the business, didn't want to hang around with women even remotely related to the business.

He had a different craving these days, for a real woman, with a *real* body and a real set of values. A woman who'd look at him and smile and melt his heart. A woman who had a life and hopes and dreams that didn't involve an Oscar or an Emmy.

He didn't care if she had her own career or logged

more miles traveling the planet than he did. He just wanted a woman who would look at him not for what he could do for her, but for what they could do for each other.

Stone always laughed at this. He didn't believe such a woman existed. Instead, he enjoyed working his way through the hordes that threw themselves at him on a daily basis.

Not Rafe. He was tired of that.

So damn tired of everything. He just needed out, in the worst possible way.

"Could we do this today?" he asked her in a voice that made her jump as much as the thunder had.

"But it's going to—" she tipped her head up again and a raindrop hit her square on the nose "—rain."

As if she'd conjured them, the drops started coming faster and harder. His associates scrambled to cover the equipment that hadn't already been protected. Instinctively, Rafe moved toward her, grabbing an umbrella to shield her hair and makeup, but as he got closer, he stopped in his tracks.

The water soaked into her hair causing it to shine in the bright spotlights. Her face went even more creamy and dewy, if that was possible. And the way the drops clung to her lashes and lips... He handed the umbrella off to a lighting tech, staring in relief at Amber. "The weather will work to our favor. Let's do this."

Amber bit her lower lip. "But I don't think—"

"Perfect. Don't think."

"Yes, but..."

Frustrated, he closed the gap between them and whipped off her sunglasses to see her eyes. If they were red or glazed over, he was going to—

Clear, light amber eyes lowered, shifted away as she again dragged her lower lip over her teeth.

And...*blushed?*

Wait a minute. Wait a damn minute. Amber had never blushed a day in her life. As a photographer, as a person who specialized in catching the secret nuances in every single thing around him, he suddenly saw the truth as clear as day.

This quiet, introspective woman was not the wild, outgoing, outrageous Amber he knew.

That meant one of two things. Either Amber had done a complete about face in the week since he'd seen her at the last shoot or...

Or this was Amber's twin sister.

What had Amber called her—Queen Emma? Yes, that was it. *Queen Emma.* He tried to remember why, but as he'd long ago learned to tune out Amber's long, meaningless, selfish ramblings, he couldn't recall.

Nor could he think of one good reason why Amber would send her sister in her stead, when this calendar was a huge career-boosting deal for her. She'd campaigned every bit as long and hard to get it as Stone had.

"Amber," he said, testing, figuring Emma would

speak up any moment now and tell him why she was here instead of her pain-in-his-ass sister.

Her gaze darted to his. "Um...yes?"

Shit. He was right. This most definitely was not Amber. "Change," he said in a low, controlling voice that would have had Amber flipping him off. "Now."

He watched in disbelief as she nodded.

She really wasn't going to tell him the truth? Ah, hell, this was bad. He didn't need this. He glanced at Stone, who again simply lifted a broad shoulder. Clearly still as mystified as Rafe.

Okay, fine, Rafe thought. Amber and Emma were identical twins; no one could tell them apart. As long as he could get his shot and have no one the wiser, he honestly didn't care why the hell either of them were playing switcheroo.

Besides, "Queen Emma" couldn't possibly be any more difficult than the notoriously difficult Amber.

"Do it," he said with another nudge toward the changing area. "The rain is good, but with you just standing there, we're wasting the little light we have left."

Seemingly, reluctant, she moved toward the bamboo poles and sheets, dragging her feet in a way Amber never would have.

Stone came up to his side, holding a light meter and a clipboard that was getting waterlogged. He was as blond as Rafe was dark, with a tough, medium build that reminded Rafe of a boxer. Stone looked as irritated as Rafe felt as they watched her go. "What's the problem?" he asked.

"Hopefully nothing."

Stone snorted his opinion of that, which made Rafe smile a bit grimly. With Amber there was always a problem, but how about with Emma?

The sheets shifted as she moved within them, and grumbling sounded on the stormy air, but she didn't call out or reappear.

"She probably needs help," Rafe said on a sigh, looking at his watch.

Stone clasped him on the shoulder. "I'll go. You'll just be tempted to kill her."

"And you won't be?"

Stone flashed a white grin. "She's in there naked. I'm never tempted to kill a naked woman."

Rafe listened to the muttering, watching the wild movements of the sheets. Amber never muttered. Nope, if that woman ever had an issue of any sort—and there were at least a million of those a day—she screamed them out for the world to deal with.

But not today.

Because it wasn't Amber, but Emma who was currently ruminating about the thin material of the costume, which, in itself, was just another dead giveaway.

Amber had a body to die for, and she lived to show it off. What did she care about the thinness of the material? All the better to expose herself.

Stone waggled a brow at him, then ventured closer

to the sheets. "Need any help?" he called out, reaching with one hand to peek in.

"No! I'm...fine. I'll be right there."

Stone glanced back at Rafe in surprise, because he also knew it was extremely unlike Amber to not require an entire posse, a minimum of ten people hovering around her, jumping to her every whim.

Then again, as apparently only Rafe realized, they weren't dealing with Amber.

Hell if he'd lose time over this. Emma would suit his purposes just fine—his purpose being to get this shoot over with.

Assuming she came out of the dressing room sometime today.

2

EMMA WILLIS STOOD NAKED, surrounded by a few flimsy sheets and bamboo poles, somewhere on the northern tip of Kauai, all courtesy of her sister Amber.

It was unbelievable that she, a known anal-retentive workaholic, had landed herself in this position. But she had and she'd have to deal with it.

Just as she'd dealt with every other Amber emergency over the years. And there'd been far too many to count.

Emma looked at the little triangular patch of white silk in her fingers that made up the bottoms of the costume. *Just put the thing on,* she told herself. But how did it go on? There was no way this would come anywhere close to covering her. Hoping against hope, she shook it out and held it up, but nothing changed.

It wasn't *meant* to cover her.

She could see now that the thin strap of silk was actually a thong.

A *thong*.

She was sure Amber Willis, actress, model and all-around hell-raiser, would love wearing such a contraption, but Emma Willis, lowly soap-opera scribe and all-around pansy, hated thongs.

Amber was going to owe her big.

She had to laugh at that. Amber *always* owed her big, and hadn't paid up once. What did that say about her, Emma wondered wildly, that she just kept saving her sister, no matter what? Far too much to contemplate at the moment, she decided, and reached for the top.

Which turned out to be even worse than the bottom.

She'd had high hopes for the filmy material because there was a lot of it, but when she placed it against her skin, she might as well have been as naked as a newborn. She supposed that was the idea of the thing. Virginal sacrifice was the theme of this shoot and she was about to look the part.

She certainly felt it. The rain drummed the sheet around her, soaking through so that water ran down the sides of the changing area. Still, the air felt refreshingly cool, not cold, and in an odd contrast, the ground beneath her bare feet was warm.

Amber had called her two days ago from some island in the Caribbean, where she'd been lounging for a few days with her latest boy toy. "This guy can give me an orgasm from the next room," she'd exhaled dreamily over the thousands of miles to Emma. "I think he's The One."

Right. The One.

There was no The One and after years of watching

Amber make a fool out of herself over and over again, Emma just wished Amber would realize it as well and stop falling in love at the drop of a hat.

Or a nicely filled-out pair of Levi's.

But before Emma could sing that old refrain and remind her sister how many times "love" had turned out to be sheer lust, the kind that always faded, Amber had begged Emma to take on this job, the one that Amber had already signed to do and had been paid for, because this calendar was going to "launch her as nothing else had."

There had been many such declarations over the years from Amber, but Emma still had such high hopes for her sister, who despite all her wildness was still her sister.

Who couldn't handle responsibility to save her life.

But Emma could, even if she couldn't see how parading half nude in filmy white material would boost Amber's acting career, when not even a bunch of real acting jobs had done that.

But love and stupidity kept Emma wishing. And hoping.

And helping.

Besides, maybe this job *would* be the one to launch Amber's career, maybe this guy *would* finally be The One. Who was Emma to decide they weren't?

And, anyway, how was this any skin off her nose? She was in Kauai, a place she'd seen only in pictures, getting drenched by the daily rain she'd wanted to see so badly. In Los Angeles, she could only dream about daily rain. And for once, she wasn't holed up in her small office, fingers cramped from all the pages she'd produced for the soap opera she wrote for.

How many times had she promised herself she'd do something fun for herself? This could be that fun. Yes, she was worried about missing two days away from her script, but they were weekend days and, theoretically, her own.

"Theoretically" because the soap opera and the studio who owned it had taken complete advantage of her over the years, and she'd let them. She worked directly beneath the head writer—a coup for any twenty-six-year-old—but the head writer was a tyrant who worked her people to the bone.

And still Emma did it, week in and week out.

Well, it was time for a little break. Hard as it was to believe, she really was going to put this itty-bitty costume on, and use her beauty instead of her brain. Just because the design was everything she wasn't, and just because being in front of a camera made her nervous, and just because she was shaking in her bare feet, didn't mean a thing.

In the name of Amber, in the name of having some of her own "fun," she'd do this.

"Let's go," came the forceful, impatient voice from the other side of the sheet.

At the sound of him, her heart leaped into her throat. She didn't have to see him to remember how potent he'd been upon first sight. He was everything Amber had said he was—tall, imposing, with a set of dark, dark eyes that she had a feeling saw just about everything. Though he'd looked unhappy to see Amber, Emma supposed she couldn't hold that against him. She knew exactly how difficult Amber could be, and imagined he had braced himself for a nightmare shoot.

He wouldn't take lightly to being fooled—if he found out. Telling him now was out of the question. Her sister had been clear on that. If Rafe knew Amber had bailed, he'd bail, too, and then the calendar would be cancelled and she'd be back to square one.

This job was a coup and she needed it.

Emma had agreed, so she stepped into the thong. She tried to adjust it, but there was no adjusting to be made. The thing was going to ride up her butt no matter what—and it did—and yet…not so bad.

Laughing at herself now, she held up the "top." Looking at it, thinking about how it would look on her, made her feel—this was such an embarrassing admission, even to herself—sexy.

Bring on the fun, she thought. She was on an island far from home with no one she ever planned on seeing again. She might as well enjoy it.

"Come on, damn it," Rafe growled from the other side of the curtain, apparently out of patience. The sheets ripped apart, leaving her staring one irritated, wet photographer in the face. All six feet two inches of him. His hair was slicked back from his forehead, his lean jaw tense as more than a few drops of water ran off his cheeks and down his throat. His plain dark blue T-shirt stuck to him like a second skin and was tucked into a pair of faded Levi's, both of which exhibited a body in its prime.

The costume was definitely getting to her if she was thinking about him that way. She hurriedly wrapped the filmy material around her torso and crossed her arms over her chest. "I'm not ready." Not sure if she ever would be, now that the moment was at hand.

"But I am."

Clearly Amber had managed to annoy him in the not-too-distant past. Emma would have to deal with that, and the fact he was startlingly handsome, so much so that he could be in front of the camera.

Except, she couldn't imagine him looking virginal.

"Not that you care, but I need the light that we're losing with each passing second." Without so much as a glance at her body—so much for the ego she hadn't even realized she had—he took her wrist and tugged her out of the protective covering of the sheets.

He walked quickly and smoothly on the rough path, forcing her to jog to keep up with him. She ran alongside while simultaneously trying to keep the material around her and her thong in place. By the time he got her to the set, she was huffing and puffing.

She really had to find the time to exercise more thoroughly than the occasional yoga tape. But she knew she wouldn't. If she wasn't writing, she was sleeping and if she wasn't sleeping, she was plotting.

Work ran her life.

Work *was* her life.

So how she'd ended up in paradise half-naked still boggled the mind, but here she was, determined to save Amber and have fun for once, with Rafe and his assistant staring at her, waiting for her to pull some model magic out of a hat she'd never worn before.

The rain still fell, big heavy drops sparse enough that they felt nice and cool landing on her hot, steaming skin. If she could have, she would have loved to take a long walk in it, alone, soaking it all in, getting drenched, cooling off—

The other man came forward as Rafe went to his camera. What had Amber told her the tall, gorgeous blonde's name was? *Stone.* Stone didn't like Amber, but her sister hadn't cared and said Emma shouldn't care, either. Now Emma wondered at that, sensing a long story behind the casually made statement, and wished she'd found out the reason for the animosity.

Stone's light blue eyes were cool but kinder than Rafe's as he pointed to the hammock. "There. Give us some good stuff quickly and we can all get out of here."

Good stuff. Right. No problem. Her skin was damp, and her hair… God knows how bad it had gotten. A woman came close and introduced herself as Jen, the makeup and hair artist.

"I'll just—" She started to play with Emma's hair, but lowered her hands when Rafe called out to her.

"She's perfect," he said, holding three film canisters. "The skin's got a fabulous glow and the hair is good. Leave it."

Odd how just those words, spoken so impersonally and not even directly to her, caused a flutter in Emma's belly.

He thought she was perfect.

Before today, it had never occurred to her to go into modeling. *You're too smart to waste your life that way,* her mother had drilled into her at a young age.

And agreeing, Emma had always been the studious one. But there was something to be said for being told she was perfect by a stranger. She wondered what her mother would think of that, as she'd never imagined her daughters perfect at all.

Emma got onto the hammock—no easy feat in itself—and pulled the material tighter around her, keeping her arms crossed over her breasts.

Stone reached toward her and Emma tried not to wince. He was going to arrange her, touch her—and this would be the hardest part. Amber loved to be touched, craved it like everyone else craved air.

Emma, however, didn't. She closed her eyes. Tried to breathe.

"Stone, where's the white umbrella?" Rafe called out from behind the camera.

"The white..." Stone looked at the blue one they'd

used earlier and swore. "In my room." He looked over the setting, the rain misting down on their model, the lighting, and sighed in agreement. "Yeah. I need to go get it, it's just what you need." He started jogging up the path Emma had just been tugged down by Rafe.

Emma turned back to the camera, but suddenly Rafe was standing right in front of her—tall, big and wet. As a few errant drops hit him they practically steamed right off his body.

"Hold still," he said.

She held still and looked into his dark eyes, watching to see if he watched her. *Saw* her.

"Relax."

No, he didn't really see her, at least not as a woman. She didn't know if she was relieved or insulted.

Relieved, she decided a minute later, realizing she'd never felt so utterly naked. Living her life as she did, with work being all she ever thought about, she wasn't used to this nude thing. She'd had the occasional relationship, but given her schedule, *occasional* was the key word. It had been a good long time since she'd had so much as a kiss and even then, since she remembered being on deadline at the time and completely distracted, it hadn't been anything to write home about.

Casual nudity had never become a part of any of those occasional relationships. She always rushed through her day, preoccupied, rarely seeing *herself* naked, much less letting anyone else see her. Being so exposed right now was like one of those dreams where she found herself on the school bus, without clothes.

It was horrifying, terrifying, mortifying—

"Perfect," Rafe said, looking through his camera at her.

Her tummy fluttered again. Her nipples tightened. And her thighs clenched. Yes, she was horrified, terrified, mortified…

And somehow excited at the same time.

"Hug your knees." He came out from behind the camera, moved close.

Ohmigod. If she weren't so bared to the cool raindrops, she might have broken out in a sweat—

Silent, brooding, he wrapped his fingers around her ankles, lifting until she bent her knees. Then he took her wrists, dragging her arms around her legs. "Bend your head down, just a little—" He sounded gruff, frustrated, so it confused her when he suddenly softened. "Oh yeah," he breathed. "Just right." He stroked her hair from her face, his fingers brushing her skin.

Her gaze jerked up to his as her nipples tightened even more, but he was completely lost in getting the pose he wanted.

She might have laughed at how impersonal it all was, except that she couldn't guarantee she wouldn't sound hysterical, so she kept it to herself.

"Set your chin on your knees," he commanded,

oblivious to her inner turmoil. ''And look directly into the camera, as if you're just a little nervous.''

A little nervous. Ha! If he only knew just how nervous she was. Her thighs were trembling now and she squeezed them tight.

''No, stay loose.''

She tried, but again he came out from behind the camera. This time he put a hand on her thigh.

Her body twitched.

''Loose,'' he commanded.

Impossible. Despite the fear and embarrassment, that excitement was humming through her insides again. At the realization, she felt her face heat. How could this be? What kind of sick woman would be excited about being naked, in front of a stranger, having him touch her, toss demands at her? She didn't know, but she couldn't deny it. She was into this, and feeling so overwhelmingly sexy that she didn't know how to handle herself.

Not paying any attention to her or her turmoil, Rafe pried the loose filmy material free of her hands and shook it out, leaving her completely bare except for the small triangle of her thong.

This was worse than the naked-in-the-bus nightmare, far worse, and at the same time somehow even more exciting, but she hunched over her knees, hugging them for all she was worth.

He handled the fabric like a pro, putting it back

around her in a way that satisfied him, and left her feeling like she sat on a high wire without a net.

And still he just looked at her.

She squirmed, and as she always did when she was out of her element, she started talking—too much. "I know, I should have done sit-ups." She crossed her arms tighter over her breasts, which were plain old B cups, but somehow in the forest, wet from the rain, they appeared closer to a C. "And a Thigh Master wouldn't hurt, either, but—"

"You're crazy." He shook his head and stepped back, assessing her before pulling her arms free of her body to drape them over her knees again as he wanted, cocking his head to study her. "You know damn well you've got a body that brings grown men to their knees."

Maybe Amber knew, but Emma rarely thought of herself that way. His praise made her nipples even happier, and her thighs were doing that funny clench and unclench thing again. She swallowed hard and stared at him, trying to get it together, but she couldn't, she just couldn't. Amber hadn't told her how incredible-looking he was, how masterful, how utterly confident. She hadn't said his touch would bring goose bumps to the surface of her flesh or that his voice would make her want to shiver.

Amber hadn't said any of those things and, as a result, Emma decided she needed to get out more.

"Hold that position," he said.

Holding. Her bent legs covered her in the front, but then he walked around the hammock, slowly, taking her in, and she could only imagine the picture she created from behind with her thong riding high—

"Hmm."

"What's the matter?" she asked shakily, resisting the urge to reach around and yank at the satin dividing her butt in a most intimate way.

"That's odd."

"What's odd?" Did she have a zit? *What?*

"I've never noticed that freckle before."

"F—freckle?"

"Yeah, this one right here—"

She nearly leaped right out of her skin when she felt the blunt tip of his finger stroke her right buttock and the freckle.

He'd never noticed it before because her sister didn't have one. "Oh. Well…it's usually covered."

"Not when I've seen you."

That deflated some of her exhilaration, oddly enough. So he'd seen her sister in far less than this outfit. She should have figured as much. And having his finger touch her so intimately shouldn't matter, either, but her entire body felt so…aware. The lightweight material brushing and teasing her breasts seemed too rough suddenly, and her over-sensitized nipples quivered at her every breath as they rubbed against the material. "M—maybe it's a new one."

"Uh-huh. From all your nude sunbathing?"

Sounded good. "Yes."

"Funny then, how creamy and pale your skin is." He came around the front again, looking over every inch of her with his photographer's eagle eye, lingering on her legs, which were up in front of her.

Could he see between them? She didn't want to know, she really didn't.

Being aroused like this was not only painful but embarrassing. As a writer she'd put her characters in situations that she'd thought sexy, but she knew now she'd been tame, and that was because she hadn't had any idea of what *sexy* really meant.

Now she knew.

Rafe was still looking at her, which made her want to squirm again. Then there was the matter of the thong, tight in front, brushing against a sensitive part of her in a shocking, tantalizing manner with every passing second until she could hardly breathe.

"Shouldn't you take the picture now?" she asked.

"Shh." He took the material again, draping the transparent length of it over her head, bringing the ends down to the hands holding her knees and slowly tucking it in. "Nice. Hold." He backed to his camera. "Holding on to the material, lift your hands and toss your head back to the sky."

"What?"

"Do it."

"But...I'll be uncovered."

''Your knees will shield your breasts from the camera.''

But what about from him? Holding her breath, trying not to picture how hard her nipples were or how her belly rose and fell with her every erratic breath, she did what he'd asked, she lifted her arms and tossed back her head.

A little.

''More,'' he commanded in that silky voice that was so utterly captivating and tyrannical at the same time. ''Expose your throat. Thrust your breasts out. Sacrifice yourself, Amber. You know you love to do that.'' He peered out from his camera and gave her a long, assessing look. ''Unless there's some reason why you wouldn't.''

Oh boy. ''Of course not.'' Breathing as if she'd been running, she ''sacrificed'' herself, throwing out her arms, tossing back her head, thrusting out her breasts, and over the roar of the blood in her ears, she heard a hiss of breath. She had no idea if it was Rafe—who else—and wasn't sure if she wanted to know because it sounded so...*primal.*

''Hold that,'' he said.

She tried not to think about how much of her he could see while she held the pose. All around her was the scent of the forest and above her came the sound of the rain.

And the clicking of his shutter.

''A little bit more.'' His voice was both low and

husky, and utterly hypnotic. "Open your eyes wide. Like that. Now your mouth, pant a little, like you're both petrified and aroused beyond belief— Yeah, just like that."

If he only knew she *was* petrified and aroused beyond belief, despite the fact that Jen and the other techs were still watching and that Stone had come back down the path holding a white umbrella in his hand—

A sharp bolt of lightning startled a gasp out of her, the following boom of thunder nearly stopped her heart and she hugged herself again, breaking out of the strange trance Rafe's voice had put her in.

Rafe took one last shot of her like that before lowering the camera. "The rain I didn't care about. But the electrical storm we'll have to wait out. I don't want to get struck by lightning. Break time," he said when she just sat there staring at him.

She stood on legs that were still a little shaky, grateful when Jen came forward with a soft, silky white robe that she wrapped around herself as quickly as she could.

"Did you get it?" Stone asked Rafe.

Emma strained to hear his answer, hoping against hope that he'd indeed gotten whatever it was he felt he'd been looking for, that the shoot was done and over with so that she could fly home to her little world of work, work and more work, with only the occasional dream about this venture into a world she'd had no idea existed.

It had been shocking, being so exposed to perfect strangers. Shocking and erotic.

Amber would laugh at that. Her sister definitely didn't consider what she did erotic, but rather manipulative. And she loved that—loved manipulating men into little panting puppies.

That didn't appeal to Emma and, now that it was over and the cameras were being set into their cases, she was trying to tell herself that she hadn't felt anything but humiliation.

But deep down, she knew the truth.

"I can't be sure," Rafe said with a frustrated shake of his wet head. "I want to come back when the storm passes."

They were coming back.

She was coming back.

3

BY THAT AFTERNOON, they all realized the storm wasn't going anywhere.

If Rafe wanted the virginal shot in the tropical forest of Kauai for the calendar—and he did—then he couldn't take the chance by leaving now. He'd have to deal with the weather and work around it.

Fine. He'd do whatever it took to finish this job, to get what he wanted. Retirement. He could indulge himself instead of dealing with other people's schedules and needs. He could ride his bike down the coast of California if he felt like it, maybe from Santa Barbara to his new home in Los Angeles, the one he'd bought three months ago and had hardly unpacked or bought furniture for. He'd catch up with old friends. He'd visit with his sisters Carolyn and Tessa, both of whom he was extremely close to.

He'd get himself a big, sloppy, happy puppy for his new place. Not exactly the wife and kids his family had been campaigning for, but he'd work on that as well.

But first up, dealing with Emma, the Amber substitute. And even though his gut said that the film he'd shot earlier would be breathtaking, he wanted more, just to be sure. With the rain now coming down in cupfuls, he stalked out to the set as the dark afternoon gave way to evening. The gazebo was empty, but he could see how she would look there on the bench, wet and dewy, surrounded by candles, glowing and just a touch nervous.

She had that last down and if anything had convinced him she wasn't Amber, it had been the look in her eyes when he'd asked her to spread her arms and toss back her head.

Amber loved exposing her body and would have done so with abandon.

Queen Emma...she clearly wasn't used to any such thing. She'd trembled and shivered, and he might have felt guilty, except that she'd come here of her own free will, for whatever reason.

It still made no sense. Why the hell didn't she tell him who she was? Did she really think she could play him?

Nobody played him.

Why would she want to?

He didn't know, didn't care as long as she did the job. He pulled out his radio and called Stone. "The lightning is gone. Let's do this."

DESPITE THE DELUGE OF RAIN, the air was hot and humid, so, that when Emma got out of the shower, she couldn't get dry. She'd been working on her laptop in her hotel room, taking her script on a wild and sexy turn she hadn't seen coming. In a way, she supposed she could thank Amber and Rafe for that. This afternoon's session had let something loose in Emma.

Then Stone had called her and told her to report back to the set, costume on. She hadn't even hung up the phone before her heart had started a heavy beat.

She was going back. Costume on. For once, her own work flew right out of her head and she had a flash of what it would feel like if the people in her world could see what she was about to do.

Amber would get a big kick out of her uptight and slightly prudish twin blushing nonstop. Her mother, a prestigious author, would probably take one look at Emma's costume and have a fatal heart attack, because in her eyes, Emma was already compromising her talents by writing for a soap opera. What was it she'd called Emma's work? Oh yes, a waste of trees.

Seeing Emma now would just confirm what she'd always known—that her daughters were some odd and inexplicable mutation of the family genes. Her mother would blame Amber, of course, citing that she'd been a bad influence from infanthood, which indeed she had. Emma had gotten really good at being in the middle of those two. If her mother ever found out about this, Emma would manage to smooth it out somehow, as she always did. But she couldn't concentrate on that now, not while looking at her costume lying innocently on the bed.

Stone had told her not to worry about her hair, that they wanted it long and loose and damp. Well, good, because that's what she had to work with at the moment—long and loose and damp. Dropping her sundress, she slid back into the thong, grimaced at herself in the mirror as she wrapped the white material across her breasts like a bandeau, and then put on the silk robe Jen had given her.

Emma still felt naked.

She glanced back at her laptop on the hotel bed, where she'd worked all afternoon. *Live And Love* had been in a ratings slump for months, and she'd tried to help fix it by putting their fan-favorite leads in romantic pairings.

But oddly enough, fans didn't necessarily want sweet, traditional romance. According to their letters—buckets and buckets of letters—they wanted steamy, hot sex. That had worried their head writer, which in turn had worried Emma a little—okay, it had worried her a lot, because she wasn't very good at steamy, hot sex. But she'd given it a shot this afternoon.

Guess that meant she could use this trip as a research tax write-off.

Holding the robe open, she took another peek at herself in the mirror. Her sexy twin looked back—a tall, willowy brunette with wild, light amber eyes and a see-through outfit that brought to mind all sorts of wicked things.

Oh boy.

With renewed anticipation, she tied her robe, slipped into her sandals and braved the storm to head toward the set.

And her evening of research.

Walking through the hotel lobby in her white silk robe, she noticed that no one even glanced her way. So much for knocking people over with her newfound sexuality. Trying to get into playing Amber, she swung her hips a little more and tossed back her hair, but only succeeded in tripping down the front stairs as she headed outside into the falling night.

The path was lit but it was still an eerie and strange feeling, walking through the heavy, drumming rain with no one accompanying her but her own thoughts. The growth beneath her feet squished like a sponge as she moved. The night seemed noisy, with the sound of rain hitting leaves and the squawk of the occasional bird combining to bring chills to her skin.

Wet now, she reached the set. Protected by the gazebo, candles flickered on the floor, the benches, even hung from the arches, sending up a warm glow, and in the middle, bent over his camera, was Rafe.

The scene took her breath. *He* took her breath. His shirt was plastered to his big, tough body, his jeans looked as if they'd been made to fit him like a soft glove, though she doubted there was an inch of softness anywhere on him.

She hadn't made a sound, and yet, he lifted his head

as she came into the clearing. His dark hair was wet and wavy, hitting just past his collar. As she watched, he lifted a hand and pushed the hair away from his face. A face that was also wet.

His expression was shuttered and, not for the first time, she wondered at what his and Amber's relationship was like. Clearly she wasn't his favorite person in the world—not even close.

"You came," he said.

She stepped beneath the protection of the gazebo. "Did you think I wouldn't?"

"Of course I did. I thought you'd make me rant and rave, or even beg, like you did in the Amazon."

The thought of this strong, proud man begging was quite the image.

"In fact, I was so sure of it, I told Stone and Jen to take their time, that you certainly would." He gestured with his head to the bench. "Let's get this over with."

"Where's the lighting?"

"The candles will provide the only lighting this time."

"It's beautiful," she said, mesmerized by the glow, by the look of concentration on his lean, rugged face. As a workaholic, she had to admit to feeling attracted to any man who felt so strongly about his work.

Or maybe it was simply the power he held over her, the power to make her do as she normally wouldn't, to bring out the sexuality and sensuality deep within her, two things she would have sworn she was lacking.

The rain was hitting the gazebo with a steady rhythm that was better than any music. With the darkening evening, a mist had rolled in, surrounding them, making her feel as though they were the only two people on the planet.

She shivered and had no idea what she felt, exactly. Fear? Nerves? Arousal?

All of the above?

He was looking at her, looking through her, or so it felt. *What does he see when he looks at me like that?* She wondered a little wildly. She hoped it was Amber.

Feeling self-conscious, she moved toward the bench, but he stopped her.

"The robe." He held out his hand for it.

Oh yeah, the robe. She began to work her fumbling fingers on the tie that she'd knotted while back in her hotel room. But now the material was wet and that, combined with the way Rafe's proximity unnerved her, meant she couldn't get the knot undone.

With a rough sound of impatience, he brushed her fingers aside, his own warm and sure, and undid the knot in record time. He didn't stop there, but tugged the robe open, then off her, and tossed it out of the way, toward an empty chair near his camera. "Loosen that," he said, nodding to the way she'd wrapped herself.

Immediately she fought the urge to cover herself

with her hands. As a woman who felt funny in a two-piece bathing suit and who always wore a bra, she simply wasn't used to being so exposed to a man, much less the great outdoors.

But neither the great outdoors nor the man cared. Rafe looked her over impassively from her long, damp and slightly tangled hair hanging over her shoulders, down her legs to her feet, which she'd slipped out of the sandals. Her body started that odd quiver thing again.

Then she thought she saw it—a flash of heat in his eyes, her only sign that she really did look good enough to pull this off.

There was some sort of forbidden excitement in that, and a sense of power as well, so that when he pointed to the bench again, she went to it.

But nothing could stop the little feeling that she was the lamb being led to the slaughter.

"Lie down," he said in that demanding, yet somehow compelling, voice that could convince a nun to sin.

She lay on her back and studied the stark white ceiling of the gazebo. The bench was a little chilly beneath her, but since her body felt so inexplicably hot, it was okay, and at least her entire backside was covered.

"Arms up, over your head," Rafe said from behind his camera, and when she complied, he lifted his head and just stared at her.

"What?" Her arms were still stretched over her head, her body laid out like a sacrifice. "No good?"

"No," he said softly. "It's good." He kept staring at her as if he couldn't quite believe it. "It's amazing, actually." He looked through his lenses. Then he took the camera off the tripod. "Arch up, just a little."

As she did, he came close, very close, shocking her when he put a knee on the bench near her hip and looked down at her through the camera from above. "*This* is the angle," he whispered, and since he seemed to be talking to himself, not her, she remained silent.

"Remember that shoot we did in Fiji, Amber?"

His voice, so close, startled her, as did the question. "Um..."

"You played that prank on me. You've always played pranks on me, hiding my unused film, unplugging the lights, using makeup to create chicken pox, but Fiji...that was what led to our first and last date."

They'd dated only once? Amber had insinuated there was much more than that. "Well—"

"You handed me your robe, and underneath it you—" He broke off with a little laugh and pulled away from his camera to look directly at her. "Well, I don't have to tell you—you remember what you did."

She only wished she did.

"You always screw with my head, knowing damn

well that when I'm on a job, I'm on it one hundred percent, no playing around.''

She had the odd urge to apologize, to somehow alleviate his frustration with her, which was silly because he was talking to Amber, not her. But knowing that didn't take away the urge.

He added a candle near her opposite hip and lit it, his eyes dark with concentration. He ran his work-roughened fingers up her outstretched arm, moving it slightly to the right, then stared down at her again. He adjusted her other arm as well, so that her fingers brushed each other high above her head. Then he slid his fingers beneath one of her knees and lifted it slightly.

Everything within her reacted to his touch in a way that shocked her. He was simply a photographer, simply a man doing his job. A man who hardly seemed to notice she was nearly nude—

He slowly rearranged the loose, white material, draping it over her torso, her belly, curling it between her hip and the candle, then over one thigh.

At the touch on her inner leg, she jerked and a sound escaped her, one that sounded...needy.

Lord, she was bad at this, bad at being cool, calm, sophisticated Amber, bad at being so blasé about what he could see of her. Her body hummed again, hummed and ached, and it made her close her eyes.

A slight breeze brought a few drops of rain to hit her face, for which she was grateful. Research. Fun.

She was doing one and having the other, she reminded herself. One weekend pretending to be wild and open and sexy. One little weekend.

But really, this had to be the *last* time she bailed Amber out of trouble.

Her mother would be happy to hear that. Unfortunately, the knowledge was little comfort to her at the moment, lying here in practically nothing.

"Your eyes need to be open for the shot," Rafe said, and when they flew open to stare at him, his shutter clicked.

People were going to *see* this—her stretched out so open and vulnerable and...bare. They were going to see it and—

"Remember New Mexico?" He was busy with his camera, not looking at her.

"Well—"

"It was our first shoot together. You were an hour late and hated your costume, so you staged that little tantrum that got me yelled at by the director."

Sounded like Amber.

"You felt so bad you kissed me when we were done." He stopped messing with his camera and looked right at her, still at her hip, still so close that now she could see that his eyes weren't just dark, dark melting-chocolate brown but had little specks of gold in them that danced in the glow from the candles.

Eyes that were now waiting for...something from her.

"You said it would be our tradition," he said. "Just you and me, and you promised to kiss me after every shoot."

Oh God.

"You always have followed through on that promise, even when I didn't want you to. So what I'm wondering now is, why haven't you kissed me yet?" His vow was low and spellbinding, his eyes so fascinating she couldn't tear hers away.

Research, she told herself. Simple research. She could lean forward, kiss him and chalk it up to the wild, sexy experience she needed for her script.

Oh, yes, it was quite the sacrifice, but she could do it. Closing her eyes, she waited. And waited.

Finally she opened them again.

Only to find his filled with amusement. "You're supposed to kiss *me,* remember?"

Right.

Oh man, Amber, you have no idea what you're asking of me…

He cocked a brow. "Problem?"

"No—" Her voice cracked, so she cleared her throat and then licked her lips. "No problem."

His gaze darted to her mouth. "You always were a tease."

That got her. Tease? Well, tease *this*…and lifting up, she went after him.

4

IF RAFE HAD HARBORED any doubts about which twin he had, they vanished now. Emma's eyes were open, wide and unsure as she moved close, and though he felt the urge to laugh at her, he didn't, because, for whatever stupid reason, he wanted the kiss.

He wanted it from Emma. Unsettling, that.

Her lips touched his, in a short, achingly sweet little kiss that was over before he could blink.

She lay back on the bench, shot him a nervous smile. "There."

"Yeah. There." He straightened and tried to collect himself, wondering why, when he'd hoped to catch her red-handed and humiliate her for this little stunt she'd pulled, he felt as though he had just won the lottery?

The storm was messing with his head. So was his need for this shoot to be over. He'd just talked on the phone to his sister Tessa, who was still in such a state of early marital bliss that it had been almost painful to hear. He was happy for her, thrilled she'd found someone to put that joy in her voice and yet, at the same time, it'd left him feeling a little...empty.

Damn.

Time to go home. Past time. "Stretch out," he demanded, forcing himself to get back to cool and distant. He looked through the lens. God, she was beautiful—the setup, the location, the outfit... Everything was just right.

He knew within two minutes he'd already gotten all the film he needed, but he shot a little bit longer, if only to keep her there sprawled out for his eyes only.

Her nipples were hard. Was she cold...or excited? With Amber he'd had a shot at guessing, but with Emma, he had no idea. He'd teased her with his comments—"remember this" and "remember that"—hoping to startle her out of this ridiculous ruse. But in the end, he'd teased himself, for Emma hadn't caved.

She did seem to be having trouble breathing and still looked a little wild-eyed, as if uncertain about what he would ask her to remember next.

It made him want to tell her Amber had come to his room for wild sex after every photo shoot.

When he finally set the camera down, she crossed her arms over her body. "Is that it?"

When he nodded, she sat up, still hugging herself. "Can I have my robe?"

He wanted to tell her to walk over and get it, exposing her hot little ass, but even he wasn't that big of a jerk. He tossed it to her.

When he had his camera in its case and she was completely covered again, he looked at her. She'd done everything he'd asked, including things he shouldn't have asked, and still a part of him wanted to push her.

"Good shoot."

With a nod, she started walking, presumably back to the hotel room she'd taken under her sister's name. He waited until she'd brushed past him before he took her arm, holding her back. "Amber."

"Y-yes?"

He'd been going to tell her they'd never really kissed, that he *knew* who she was, but she looked so sweet, so damn unexpectedly sweet, that he got mad all over again.

Walk away, said a little voice. *You don't care. You're one shoot closer to done. Just walk away.*

"Rafe?"

"Nothing." He let her go, and turned away.

"'Night."

"'Night."

By the time he got back to the hotel, she was nowhere to be seen. Just as well.

And when he checked out early and caught a late flight back to Los Angeles, he figured he'd never see her again.

Also, just as well.

EMMA WORKED THE ENTIRE NEXT WEEK around the clock. She'd figured it would be hard to forget Kauai and all that had happened there, but her writing distracted her.

Her writing always did. She nearly forgot to eat and sleep when she buried herself. Well, she nearly forgot to *sleep*, anyway, because, quite honestly, there was little that could make her forget to eat.

Not even one tall, dark and mouthwatering photographer with a voice that made her pulse leap and a touch that had nearly kicked her heart right out of her chest.

He hadn't a clue, of course. Which made it worse, somehow. Was she *that* deprived of a man's touch that his professional one could send her skittering toward orgasm?

Yes, she had to admit, she was that deprived and it had been self-inflicted. Her work was her life and she'd always told herself it was all she needed.

Still was, she assured herself.

And yet, if it had truly been just work for him, why had he wanted that kiss? Her heart leaped again, as she remembered how warm and firm and yummy his mouth had felt on hers.

Nope, she wasn't going to go there, wasn't going to think about him and what the weekend had done to her. How he'd gotten her into the smallest thong on the planet, how she might or might not have blown her cover.

Was it possible he'd guessed the truth?

She had no idea.

But if she thought about it too much, the suspense would kill her, so she didn't think about it. Besides, what did it matter? She wasn't going to see him again.

The week went fast. When she wasn't at the studio making daily last-minute changes on the script for the network Powers-that-be, or in story meetings and staff meetings, she was at home, in her little house in the hills of Laurel Canyon, fingers pounding out page after page on her laptop, ignoring everything and everyone around her.

She had quite the new theme going for her story-lines and it excited her so much that she spent most of her time at the keyboard alternating between grinning like an idiot and fanning her hot face as the pages flew out of her.

Apparently Kauai, and everything that had happened, had inspired her.

Ironic that she could thank Amber for helping her for once, however unintentionally. She'd definitely shaken up all the main characters on her show, putting more steamy sex into one week's worth of stories than she'd put in all year. Her head writer was going to love it. The *viewers* were going to love it.

She'd even proposed introducing a new main character, a tall, dark and gorgeous photographer who had a voice of silk and a way with his hands—

The phone ringing at her side had her jumping a little and she laughed at herself when she picked it up, assuming it would be someone from the studio to yell, cajole or plead—

"Hey, sis."

"Amber," Emma said in surprise. "Boy do I have a lot to say to you."

"Really? I heard Kauai was a big hit." She sounded like she was amused.

She was always amused. Amber had that gift, she could find the humor in anything, even when life handed her a bowl of sour grapes, which it had often enough.

"I got word that those shots you took in my place are going to be the best of the bunch so far."

Not a "thank-you," not a "great job," but then, Amber wasn't known for her gratitude. "I wish you'd been more forthcoming with the details of the shoot." Emma thought of that filmy white wrap and how many people probably had looked at those shots so far, including Rafe, and felt her face heat.

"If I'd been more forthcoming," Amber said, "you wouldn't have covered for me, and I needed you."

"You always need me."

"Oh, Emma. You have no idea what I'm going through."

"Of course not, because I don't have a life."

"I didn't mean it like that."

"Look..." Emma pinched the bridge of her nose. "All I'm saying is, you could have told me I'd have to put on a skimpy little nothing."

"It was a modeling job. Every modeling job is a skimpy little nothing."

For Amber, maybe, but pointing that out would just cause a fight, and frankly, Emma didn't have the energy to spare. The fact was, Amber counted on her because Emma always came through, always took care of everything, and this time, she'd done just that. So she sighed and forced a smile.

"How's your trip?"

"Perfect. Ricardo is a dreamboat. We went skydiving today, and tomorrow we're going snorkeling. He just loves it when I put on my bikini and snorkel. But speaking of my trip..." Amber paused.

Not good. Amber was up to something, which never worked out well for Emma. "You know what? I don't mean to cut this short, but I'm in the middle of a scene..." She clicked her fingers over the keyboard as if typing. "So, I've really got to run—"

"You're always in the middle of a scene. In fact," Amber said on a laugh, "you work way too hard, sweet sister of mine. Way too hard."

Something Amber had never bothered to notice before. Emma went on full alert.

"And you know what else? You never take time for yourself. You spend all of your time at your computer or at the studio with some ungrateful executive yelling at you. That's just not right, Em, you know it isn't."

True, but at the moment, she couldn't concentrate

on anything except why her sister suddenly had taken notice of her work habits.

"That's why I wanted to give you the Kauai job," Amber said. "So that you could have some time away—"

"Whoa." Emma leaned back in her chair. "Let's review the facts. I went to Kauai for *you.* Okay? Because you called me in tears over this new guy, this new The One guy you couldn't stand to lose. You said your career counted on this job and you couldn't back out, but if you didn't go to the Caribbean with Ricardo, you were going to lose him. So I caved, I went to Kauai and posed for those pictures to help you. *Not* for time off, because I didn't actually take time off. I brought my computer—"

"You didn't!" Amber laughed. "What am I saying? Of course you did. What are you working on for the soap right now? Something good? A murder, or some pivotal character realizing he's bisexual— No, I know! A housewife has an epiphany—she hates her kids and her husband, right?" Amber laughed again. "You know what I think? You should just have everyone get into one big sex-fest. A big orgy. That'll take care of all the ratings concerns I've been reading about in *Soap Digest*—"

"We're doing just fine," Emma said defensively. "That report was biased because they like ABC's shows better."

"I just think hot sex would help, that's all. Shake the show up a little. You should try it."

"Well, funny you should say that..." Emma entwined the phone cord in her fingers. "Because in Kauai I came to the same conclusion."

"What was it, the exotic location or the fabulous cabana boys?"

Your photographer.

"A combination," she said safely, and put Rafe Delacantro right out of her mind.

Amber put him right back in it. "And the photographer and his assistant, I'll bet. Neither of them are exactly dogs, are they? Oh man, when I first laid eyes on Rafe, I swear he made my hormones stand up and beg." She laughed. "And Stone isn't a slouch in the looks department, either, for all that he's gay."

"What?"

Amber sighed. "I know, such a waste. But one night at a party, I came on to him and he declined."

"That doesn't make him gay, Amber."

"Of course it does."

Emma sighed.

"So about my trip..."

"What about it?" Emma's wariness was back.

"I was wondering how you felt about Joshua Tree National Park."

"Huh?"

"Joshua Tree. The desert just east of you?"

"I know where it is, I was just trying to figure out why you're asking me how I feel about it."

"Yeah, see, I thought maybe you'd want to go. Maybe experience the great outdoors a little more, and while you were there—"

"Amber—"

"—you could maybe just pose for a few more pictures in my place. Tomorrow. They're shooting April there."

"Oh, no—"

"It won't affect your work," Amber said quickly. "It's just Saturday. One day."

"Amber, I can't be you again." She thought a bit desperately of filmy white costumes and being in front of the camera when she hated being in front of the camera, not to mention the strange and inexplicable yearning she couldn't seem to handle when she was—

"Rafe will be taking the pictures—"

"He's going to figure it out, Amber."

"No, he won't. Look, people see what they want to see. And when they look at me, they see a beautiful, but slightly empty brunette who's good at one thing and one thing only—posing for pictures. You could do that blindfolded. You could, Emma. You have so much more talent than anything I've ever had."

"That's not true. Your job is hard, too, in a different way than mine." Characters forgotten, Emma pushed her laptop away. Elbows on her desk, she rubbed her temples and bit back a sigh. "Why can't *you* do it?"

"Well, I'm still in the Caribbean with Ricardo, and—"

Ah, yes, Ricardo. "Can't you just put Rafe off for a few more days? I mean, why did you sign up for this job in the first place if you want out of it so badly?"

"For the money, for starters." Amber sighed lustily. "I'll share it with you, I promise. But it's more than the cash. This calendar is studio distributed. It's going to be everywhere, Emmie. Everywhere. It'll be just the push I need to get a good series or movie this season, I just know it."

"Then, come back," Emma said, pitifully close to begging. No one wanted her sister to be successful more than she did. Because if Amber got successful, or at least happy, she'd stop leaning on Emma so much.

Emma could almost hear her mother laughing at that hope. No, Margaret Willis didn't have much faith in her daughters, either of them, but especially Amber. Emma had no idea if that was because her daughters were so incredibly different from her, in both looks and temperament, or if it was simply that she regretted having children so young and being held back from her career.

In any case, it had been a difficult upbringing. At least Emma used her brain, Margaret often said, having no idea that Emma had chosen to use her brain rather than her beauty simply to please the woman it turned out couldn't be pleased. Her mother had been so hard on Amber over the years that Emma—the oldest by three minutes—had always felt the need to step in and mediate.

Twenty-six years and she was still doing it.

"Please, Emma? Please won't you do this for me? Do this so I don't have to come home right now."

"Why did you let me think that you and Rafe had a past together?"

"We do."

"One date isn't a 'past.'"

Amber laughed. "Silly me, I probably had a crush on him at the time. Truth is, he wasn't into me. He's not into models or anything else Hollywood."

"So why do you kiss him after each shoot?"

"What?"

Emma was getting a bad feeling here. "So you... don't kiss him?"

"Of course not. Look, maybe I dated him that one time and maybe I like to mess with him on the set sometimes, but if I was going to kiss anyone, it would be Stone. I mean, my God, have you seen his eyes? If he wasn't gay..."

"But Rafe—"

"He's far too into his camera."

Code for he wasn't into Amber enough, of course.

So he'd gotten a kiss out of Emma under false pretenses.

What did that mean?

"So, will you do it, Emma? Go as me?"

"No. What's the costume?"

"Camper girl," said Amber. "It'll be full coverage, no doubt. Jeans and a tank, something like that. *Please?*"

Full coverage, nothing sheer, nothing so outrageously sexy that her every nerve ending quivered.

"*Please.*"

No. "I don't know..."

"You won't regret this," Amber said in a rush. "You're the best. I'll give Rafe's assistant the number where they can reach you. You posing as me, of course."

"But I didn't say I'd—"

The dial tone sounded in her ear.

"—do it," she finished, then she hung up and stared out the window of her house to the yard she'd neglected so badly that it had become nothing more than overgrown bush. She'd meant to get out there this year, but something had always come up. Work related, of course.

But now here she was taking off her second weekend in a row—unheard of—and, instead of doing something she wanted, she was saving her sister's tush.

Or was she? Because deep down, she had a feeling maybe this was what *she* wanted to do.

The phone rang again. "Oh, thank God," she said, yanking it up to her ear. "Look, I can't do it, I—"

"Amber?"

Even though she'd only heard him that one day in Kauai, she'd know that low, almost unbearably sexy voice anywhere.

Rafe.

5

"AMBER," RAFE SAID into his cell phone, which he held in the crook of his neck so his hands were free. "Tomorrow's shoot. Desert. Be there."

He had carpet samples spread across his patio table—one he'd picked up at some little shop on Melrose because the intricate inlaid wood carving on the tabletop and chairs intrigued him.

He couldn't wait to buy a barbecue and cook out here, then eat at this very table. Realizing Amber hadn't said anything, he prepared for battle. "Problem?"

He hoped not, because he wanted to hang up and match the paint samples to his carpet samples, and then get himself to the hardware store to make it a reality. He'd been told to hire a painter but he wanted to do it himself. He wanted to get his hands dirty fixing up his own house.

His house.

Damn if that didn't have a nice ring to it.

"Amber?"

"Yes—" She cleared her throat and the slightly

nervous little sound had his eyes narrowing. ''I'm... here.''

Christ, not again. Not Emma. He opened his mouth to demand answers, then shut it. He only had this one job left, then he was done. *Finito.* Finished. In light of that, he didn't want to hear what the hell Amber and Emma were up to. He didn't want to hear anything. He was tired of the game, tired of all of it.

But honest to God, he didn't know if he could handle Emma again. It wasn't the long flowing hair or the willowy, curved body and outward beauty. Hell, he was used to beauty—his world was swamped with it. And he'd seen Amber's body enough that he should also be immune to Emma's curves.

But what had drawn him about Emma went beyond skin deep. In her eyes had been a host of things that made him curious, and lurking behind her nerves had been a woman he wanted to know more about. Photographing Emma had been an experience like...like making love to a virgin. Intoxicating, exhilarating and...

Shockingly arousing.

He'd put his heart and soul into those pictures with her—more than he'd done in years—and it had thrown him. All damn week now he'd been wondering about walking away from this life of photographing others, because Kauai had been sheer and simple joy.

''I'll be there,'' she said. ''I won't forget.''

''Good.'' For one idiotic moment he wondered what

else he could say, how he could keep her on the phone, how he could get a promise out of her, but then he came to his senses. ''Thank you,'' he said, and hung up.

''So which twin is it going to be this time?'' Stone came through the sliding glass door carrying two beers, one of which he handed over before he sank to a chair. ''Diva Amber or Queen Emma?''

''Emma.''

Fascinated by this tale of twins, Stone had looked into one Emma Willis. He'd discovered that she was part of a team of soap opera writers for *Live And Love,* with a reputation for being all work and no play.

She was Hollywood, firmly entrenched there, the one place Rafe wanted out of.

He twisted the cap off his beer and tossed back his head for a long pull on the cold brew.

''Interesting.'' Stone put his feet up on the table, rolling his eyes when Rafe pushed them off. ''This whole twin thing. They should do a shoot together, something without clothes, of course—'' He broke off when Rafe snarled. ''What? I'm just wondering.''

''Go wonder about one of your beach bunnies.''

''Hey, this is Amber I'm talking about. Amber drives you insane and tells everyone I'm gay. So why would you care if I—'' He broke off, going from confused to speculative. ''Damn.''

''What?''

''She got under your skin, in just one day.''

"Amber never gets under my skin."

"I'm not talking about Amber—she could get under the skin of an elephant. I'm talking about Emma."

"Well, I'm not."

"You dated Amber once and didn't sleep with her," Stone said. "Are you never going to sleep with Emma, either? Let me know, man, and I'll stop picturing her in that thong."

Rafe glared at his friend, who laughed and stood, pulling off his shirt, leaving him in knee-length, sunshine-yellow swim trunks. "I think it's time for a swim. Why don't you call your gorgeous sisters over here so I can have some bikini scenery to keep me company?"

"Don't make me hurt you," Rafe said seriously. "And besides, Tessa's taken now."

"That leaves Carolyn. Tell her to wear that white two-piece she's got, because the water's chilly, and—" He halted with a laugh when Rafe growled at him. "Hey, it was worth a shot."

"I've got a shot for you."

"Jeez. Talk about being an overprotective older brother. I can't ogle Carolyn and you won't let me even think about Tessa. The least you can do is indulge my Amber-Emma fantasy."

"Swim, Stone. *Swim.*"

Was he overprotective? Yeah, probably. But even before his parents had retired to Florida a few years back, he and his sisters had been close. They went to each other for money, support, friendship—whatever was needed.

He relished the relationship, but at the moment felt far more disturbed at the possibility that Stone had some interest in Emma.

Rafe watched him dive into the pool and start swimming laps. Would Stone go after her? And why did it matter?

It didn't. Instead, he concentrated on the carpet samples, but his doorbell rang, the sound wafting through the open sliding glass door. Walking through his unfurnished living room into the foyer, he found a teenage kid standing at his front door.

"Hey, mister, is this cat yours?"

Rafe looked down. At the kid's feet sat the ugliest brown and gray cat he'd ever seen. In spite of the way its fur was matted and filthy, the thing lifted its chin regally and stared at Rafe from eyes so pale a blue they looked like glass. Never having been a cat person, he easily shook his head.

"Nope. Not mine."

"You sure? He's been wandering around but seems to know your place."

The cat kept his gaze over Rafe's shoulder as if it couldn't care less what the humans around it thought.

"I'm sure," Rafe said.

The kid shrugged and started to walk away.

"Hey, you're not going to just leave it here."

"It's a cat," the kid called back. "It'll go wherever it wants."

Rafe stared at the cat, who made a big production out of yawning. "Go home," he said.

The thing didn't budge.

The house across the street had recently sold and a woman stood on the end of the driveway watching him. She was tall, and had her red hair piled on top of her head. She wore a short-sleeved pink sweater and floral capris with pink sandals, and, in keeping with the Suburban in her driveway, she seemed to personify a soccer mom, albeit a hot-looking one. When she saw him looking at her, she crossed the street toward him.

"Is that a stray cat?" she asked him, looking worried.

"It's a stray something."

"Oh, the poor thing." She kneeled next to the cat and stroked it. "Poor homeless thing. What are you going to do about him?"

Rafe had planned on going back into his house and shutting the door but found he couldn't do that with her watching him. "Are you my new neighbor?"

"Oh!" She smiled and offered him a hand. "Yes, I'm Irena Dotriana, part-time interior designer, part-time mom."

"Part-time mom?"

"I share my kids with my ex-husband." She shot him a smile. "So...do you have an ex-wife?"

He laughed. ''No.''

''A not-so ex-wife?''

''Nope.''

Her smile widened just a little. ''Well, then. Need a designer?''

''I just might.'' They chatted for a few more minutes, with Rafe promising to contact her soon for ''designing'' purposes, and when she left, the cat was still there.

''What's this?'' Stone came through the house, rubbing a towel over his wet head, not bothering to dry off the rest of him so that he left a trail of wet footprints.

Rafe groaned. ''You won't be doing that once I get my carpeting in.''

''Yes, Mom.'' Stone eyed the cat. ''That's the ugliest cat ever.''

Rafe took another look at the feline, who sat as if it were royalty, while its fur stuck up in some places and was matted in others. ''Go get me a can of tuna.''

''If you feed it, you'll never get rid of it.''

''His ribs are sticking out. If I feed it, I think he'll go away.''

Twenty minutes later they were in the backyard again, with the cat at Rafe's feet.

''Told you not to feed it,'' Stone said, eyes closed, face tilted up to the sun.

Rafe glanced at the cat, whose eyes were slits.

"He's just going to take a nap. He'll leave after that. You know how cats are."

Stone shook his head. "There's a sucker born every minute."

Maybe, but Rafe had never been anyone's sucker. Or so he told himself, all the way up until the next morning, when the cat still hadn't left.

But Rafe had to. At dawn, he kicked the cat out to the front porch and drove his Jeep a couple of hours to the designated meeting spot for the day's photo shoot.

Joshua Tree National Park was one of his favorite spots to photograph. Something about the stark, barren landscape drew him, made him itch for his camera. He parked near the other cars already there.

Sitting in a chair beneath an umbrella, getting her hair worked on and her face done, was his model for the day. A miracle. She still wore her own clothes, or what he assumed were her own clothes—jeans and a zippered, hooded blue sweatshirt.

She looked like Amber.

Her eyes were closed, her face in a relaxed expression, but her body sat tensely in the chair and her hands were fisted on the armrests.

Not Amber.

Ignoring both Emma and the odd and inexplicable tug on his gut at the sight of her, he turned his back on the scene and studied the land. He'd been out here many, many times, the most recent being two weeks ago when he'd come to hunt down the specific spot for this shot.

Joshua Tree National Park was a strange and beautiful place. They were only a couple of hours east of Los Angeles, and yet they might as well have been on another planet. Instead of concrete, glass and brick as far as the eye could see, wide open, high desert prevailed, outlined with sharp, rocky mountains. He couldn't wait to shoot it, to capture the vast open space, the wild, eerie cactuslike Joshua trees.

People said Los Angeles was sex personified. But to Rafe, this place, with the wild primroses and sunflowers peeking out of the rock formations or springing from the base of the ghostly Joshua trees, with the violent, unpredictable weather and the biggest sky he'd ever seen, beat out Los Angeles for sexy any day.

From where he stood, he could see the exact place he wanted to set up. It appeared to be a large rock formation, jagged and pointing to the sky. It was only about two hundred yards away, and from his last visit, he knew it wasn't a tough climb by any means. In fact he knew which trail would take them nearly to the top. He figured he could get his model up there, standing on the point of an outcropping with the open space sprawling behind and below her, so that she would appear to be on the very edge of the earth.

Perfect.

And when he finished with the shoot, he could say he was a third done with this, his last job.

Even more perfect.

"FINISHED," JEN SAID.

Emma opened her eyes. "Thanks." She reached for her bag, wanting to write down all the script changes that had come to her while she'd been sitting there. She had no idea how Amber handled all the idle time. It would drive her crazy.

When she'd finished, she looked up and started to smile at Jen, but caught sight of herself in the mirror. "Oh my God."

Jen smiled. "You look terrific, don't you think? Hot and sexy, but innocent somehow, too. You've got such great hair, Amber."

Amber sure did. Emma's wasn't quite as thick and pampered, but apparently Jen hadn't noticed.

Which made her feel like a big jerk. "Thanks." She took one last look at the artfully messy hair, her huge eyes and lightly glossed lips. She couldn't decide if she looked like she'd just gotten into bed, or out of it. "Um...what comes now?"

"You put on your outfit."

Terrific.

"I left it in the changing area." Jen pointed to another makeshift bamboo-and-sheet dressing area. "You know...don't take this the wrong way...but you're really easy to work with lately."

She said this with such surprise, Emma nearly grimaced. Amber had gotten herself quite the reputation. "Thanks." She glanced over at the hanging sheets, wondering what would be waiting for her this time, wondering if she'd have any free minutes between now and camera time to work on the laptop in her bag; she needed to fix a scene she was worried about. She looked around, then felt someone staring at her. Craning her neck, her eyes collided with Rafe's.

His gaze was dark, inscrutable. He gave nothing away, this man, at least nothing that he didn't want to give away.

Was he thinking about the kiss? Because she was. Why had he wrangled one from her when Amber would know they didn't normally do such a thing?

Because he knew she wasn't Amber?

Her pulse skipped a beat at that, but he revealed nothing as he looked at her. He appeared the same as he had in Kauai—full of carefully restrained energy. He wore faded Levi's, the fibers white in all the stress points, of which there were many, and a cream cable-knit sweater shoved up at the elbows. He looked lean and rugged and more than slightly annoyed. Her pulse tripped again.

She wished she'd told Amber no. If she'd refused, she'd be hard at work right this very moment, lost in a script she controlled instead of wondering what was going to happen.

He gestured ahead of him, where she could see a

dusty trail leading off to what looked like a daunting mountain. Everyone around her—Stone, Jen and two lighting techs—started off, carrying whatever it was they would need.

Emma felt her mouth drop open a little. They were…taking a hike?

Rafe let out a grim smile. "You're going to want to change now—there'll be no privacy at the top."

The top. She craned her neck to even see the top. The mountain looked gigantic, dark red and extremely…sharp. Good God. She swallowed hard. Hiking wasn't her thing. Anything aerobic wasn't her thing. Give her a nice, stress-relieving yoga tape any day.

"I don't hike."

His grim smile didn't falter. "I'm not surprised, but this isn't a hike, it's just a little walk. You're not afraid of a little walk, are you…*Amber?*"

The way he said her sister's name made her glance at him, but he'd slid on a pair of dark sunglasses with reflective lenses, so she couldn't begin to tell what thoughts were running in his head.

"Do you need help changing?" he asked softly.

"No," she said. Or squeaked. She whirled away and hid behind the hanging sheets. A narrow full-length mirror hung off the bamboo, and hooked on to it was a pair of jean shorts and a bright-red halter top. On the floor sat a pair of thick wool socks and brand-spanking-new hiking boots in her size.

Not bad, she thought, letting out a breath of relief she hadn't realized she'd been holding. She'd be fully covered. She liked that, because the thought of facing Rafe in the light of day with anything less than a full set of armor felt a bit...daunting.

She stepped out of her own jeans and top, and then pulled on the shorts.

Uh, oh.

"Problem?"

She jumped a little at the sound of Rafe's voice just outside the dubious protection of the sheets, and hurriedly slipped on the halter top.

"Amber?"

She stared at herself in the mirror wondering who the hell was staring back. Certainly it wasn't her with the piles of makeup designed to appear "natural," the artfully messy hair and the eye-popping clothes, because she'd never looked so naturally...hot. Maybe it was the way Jen had teased her hair, making it seem as if she'd just stumbled out of her lover's bed—although, no one really looked this good in the morning.

And the outfit... "Man, oh man," she whispered just as Rafe pulled back the sheet.

Standing behind her, he slowly pushed the sunglasses to the top of his head. His eyes met hers in the mirror, then traveled down, over the red halter top that left her shoulders bare. It also exposed plenty of cleavage all the way to the middle of her torso and that's pretty much where the top ended. Her belly rose and fell far more quickly than she would have liked as his gaze dropped lower, to the hip-hugging shorts that were so low, the black elastic band of her panties showed around the top.

She didn't want to think about what else showed. She'd thought the thong last week had produced a wedgie beyond belief, but that was nothing to the feel of the denim riding up and exposing at least half of each cheek. She'd peek, but she didn't want to bring it to his attention—

"It's good," he said, his voice even.

How did he do that? Remain so cool, while her heart threatened to burst right out of her chest just from seeing him look at her. "There's...not a lot of coverage."

His gaze cut down to her behind. "Nope."

She stared at herself in the mirror, careful not to look at his reflection—his sharp eyes, his lean unshaven jaw or the way the wind had tousled his hair into a mess that her fingers suddenly itched to touch.

Clearly, she had lost her mind.

But it was hard to keep it when he was a mere inch behind her, when she could feel his breath on her neck, when she was watching him watch her. Even as she thought it, her nipples puckered into two tight buds.

Terror, she told herself. It was the terror at being in front of a camera again, exposed. At his beck and call.

But even as she thought it, she didn't believe it.

No, what she felt wasn't terror, but…excitement. Arousal.

And she had no idea what to make of that. Or of herself.

6

IN THE END, Rafe had to hold her hand. It was that or lose her on the last leg of the climb to the top of the rock formation, and he used the word *climb* loosely.

Really, it'd been nothing more than a slightly taxing walk. But not to his model. "Let's go," he said over his shoulder, practically towing her. The sky was wide open and so blue he could have drowned in it, but that was only directly overhead. From the west came a rather vicious wind and he could see the white clouds darkening as they swirled together and gained momentum.

How many times had he been here? he wondered. The rocks, the sky, the amazing foliage that survived the harsh winters and violent summers…it all amazed and calmed him in a way little else did.

But his experience told him what those clouds meant. He knew they might have an hour before the unexpected spring storm hit…or five minutes. "Come on."

She blew a strand of hair from her face. "'Come on,' he says," she muttered, and used her free hand to yank at the jean shorts that couldn't possibly be yanked at because there simply wasn't enough material. "I'm coming, I'm coming."

Coming. Such an innocent word, really, so why it put a picture in his brain of her sprawled out and naked beneath him, *coming,* he had no idea.

He shook his head and strove to find something else to think about. "I thought you've been running and taking yoga," he said. Emma vexed and puzzled him, so he felt like vexing and puzzling her back.

"Running?"

Apparently the twins did have at least one thing in common—a healthy dislike of strenuous exercise. "You know, jogging? To keep fit?"

"Oh. Yes."

He glanced at her in time to see her worry her lower lip, and bit back his own grim smile. He really had no idea why he loved torturing her, but he wasn't nearly done. "Because I have to tell you, Amber, you need to get a refund on that private trainer you hired."

When the wind whipped up her hair and blew it across her face, she irritatedly shoved the hair away. "She's, um, been on vacation."

"You mean 'he?' *He's* been on vacation?"

Dismayed, she just looked at him.

The cost of her clothing—$150.

The price of her makeup and hair—$200.

The look on her face—priceless.

"Yes," he said. "You remember Harris. The trainer you use four times a week."

"Clearly," she said, and she managed a laugh. "I shouldn't walk and talk at the same time."

He couldn't help it, he laughed, too. Poor baby, being so torn between having to lie and needing to keep the cover—God only knows why.

And damned if he wasn't attracted to her innocence even as the continued lie bugged the hell out of him.

Somehow it combined, in some weird way, to work as a powerful aphrodisiac. It was sick, he knew, being turned on by her under the circumstances and he knew he had to ignore it.

And her.

At least, the best he could. Luckily, they reached the top. He admired the view and took a deep breath, but when he turned to her, he let the breath out with a laugh.

Bent, hands on her knees, she huffed and puffed for air. "Don't say a word."

"Word."

She laughed. "Why do you do that? Why are you so..."

"So...?"

"So tough? Hard to crack?"

He just looked at her and her open expression shuttered.

"You know, there's something I'd really like to tell you," she said. "But it's complicated."

"Why?"

"Because I *can't* tell you."

"That doesn't make much sense, *Amber.*" He emphasized her name, and she winced a little.

"I know."

Above them, the clouds were moving like a speeding train. He didn't want to have to bail back to the cars and sit and wait out another storm. "What are the chances you're going to tell me the thing that you can't tell me?"

"Small," she said apologetically. Her eyes were filled with conflict. "I promised I wouldn't."

"Tell me, anyway."

"I have a better idea. Let's just do this."

Fine. "Wait here." He went to the edge where he wanted her to stand during the shoot. In spite of the whipping wind, Stone had set up already, and with the lighting perfect, they were ready.

"Now's better than later," Stone said, checking his light meter. "I don't think we have a later."

Rafe glanced upward, watched the clouds rumbling. Yep, they were losing time quickly. He looked back at Emma. She was bent over again, and he took a moment to take in the nice view of the hot shorts riding up her—

"Now, *that's* the shot that would sell millions," Stone said in appreciation. "She should bottle that ass and—" He broke off when Rafe growled. "What?"

"She's our *model.*"

"Right. I think I know that." Stone eyed him. "Don't look now, man, but you're doing it again."

He waggled a knowing eyebrow. "Just like last week. You're acting like you're interested in her beyond how she looks through your lens."

"And you're doing it again."

"What's that?"

"Talking too much."

Stone just laughed. "So…when are you going to tell her we know she's not Amber?"

Stone took another look at Emma. She straightened and swiped at her brow, then grimaced and checked her arm, presumably to see if she'd smeared her makeup. She had, he could see from here, and she sent a sweet smile of apology to Jen, who rushed over with her bag.

Amber never would have apologized, nor would she have wiped her face on her forearm. Because, at all times, Amber was intensely aware of her makeup and how she looked.

Clearly, Emma wasn't.

He waited until she'd been repaired, waited until she stood alone near the edge of the rock formation. Near the edge and yet far back. Apparently she was trying to look and trying not to look at the same time, while casually glancing around her to see if anyone was watching her.

As well as being unused to a lot of makeup, Emma didn't like heights.

And she obviously didn't like being so exposed. Her hair was still whipping around her face, and through the halter top he could see her nipples puckering against the material...just before she crossed her arms over her chest and hugged herself.

For the oddest reason, that got him, and he moved to her side, blocking her from view of the others. "Cold?"

She shrugged.

Not a complainer, he'd give her that. "Beautiful, isn't it?"

Startled, she glanced at him as if not sure what he was referring to. When she saw him looking out to the desert beyond them, she relaxed a little.

"I never would have imagined, but it is. The Joshua trees look like tall, skinny old men."

"You should see them in winter. Once in a great while it snows. Then they look like tall, skinny old women."

She laughed and the sound tugged at the corners of his mouth until he found himself smiling back at her.

Their gazes and the humor connected them, and then their smiles slowly faded but they didn't stop looking at each other. He could see the pulse at the base of her neck kick into gear and he knew how she felt because his own had started cooking, too.

He'd been around beautiful women for years now, and somehow, at some part, he'd grown immune. Not that he'd stopped seeing them or acted like a monk, because he surely hadn't. But it seemed that the more time went by, the less he felt moved by any particular woman.

It was all tied up with his need to stop doing this kind of photography, to settle down and find one woman, the one who could excite him for the rest of his life.

Which meant he had to finish this shoot. ''Ready?''

''Here,'' Stone said, pointing to her mark. Next to it was an ancient-looking rock formation—three large rocks, one on top of another so that they stood just slightly below the height of her shoulders. ''Lean on them,'' he instructed her. ''Toss your head back, with your hair over one shoulder so we can see the line of your spine.''

And her ass. Rafe could see that thought flash through her mind and he contained his grin at her look of dismay. Maybe she'd tell him right now. His smile vanished because he couldn't believe how much he wanted that, wanted her to confess to him.

Instead she stepped onto her mark, put her hands on the rocks and arched her back, just a little, and with the beautiful and eerie desert as her background, and with her long brunette hair flowing over one shoulder, she looked back at him.

Her skin looked positively luminous, the red halter only emphasizing her willowy yet curvy form. Her legs were so long that they exceeded the legal limit, and capping them off with hiking boots had been a stroke of genius. She looked like a wild, yet innocent, sex goddess and he knew every pair of eyes that took in this picture would want her.

He wanted her.

He looked at her through the lens. No doubt the shot would be another incredible one. "Cock one hip, just a little—"

Almost before the words were out, she did it and hit the right pose. Except, she wasn't looking at him; she was looking down, as if she *couldn't* look at him. He knew her big secret was killing her.

"Amber...you've got to look at me."

"I know." She closed her eyes, then opened them on him. "I'll never forget today," she said softly. "I know I was a pain getting up here, but my God—" she looked out to the view and slowly shook her head in awe "—it's...life altering."

He adjusted his focus through the lens. "In what way?"

"It's so...big. So...real life. It makes all my problems seem so small."

"Yeah? Smile just a little, mostly with your eyes, there you go..." He focused a little closer...*perfect,* it was perfect. "What kind of problems do you have?"

She laughed. "Oh boy. If you only knew." She looked around her again and sighed. "I just can't get over how incredible it all is."

"Because you've never seen it."

"I've never seen anything like it."

Aw, hell. He was going to tell her. "You've been here before."

Her gaze flew to his.

"Or at least Amber has."

And while she stood there speechless, looking gorgeous and just a little bit off kilter, he got his shot. He clicked his shutter until he was out of film then he slowly nodded. "Several times, in fact. She's been here and she hated every moment of it—the drive, the heat, the dryness, every insect that had the bad misfortune of landing on her. She hated every cactus, every single Joshua tree. She hated all of it."

Emma stared at him, eyes widening and then shutting for a moment.

He waited her out and when she opened her eyes again they were drowning in regret.

"I'm sorry. I'm so sorry."

"You're Emma."

"You knew." She looked shocked to the bone. "When did you figure it out?"

"About two minutes after you walked onto the set in Kauai."

"But how? How did I give it away?"

"It was what you didn't do." He ticked the reasons off on his fingers. "You weren't demanding things and you weren't trying to hit on every single man around…"

"Oh."

"I looked into your eyes and saw Emma. Queen Emma."

"Queen..." She sputtered, making him laugh. "*Queen* Emma?"

"Amber always refers to you as that. You didn't know," he said and laughed again. "Honestly, I think she actually means it as a compliment."

"Right." She blew a strand of hair away from her face, then let out a little disparaging sound. She stared at him some more. "You never said anything, you never gave it away that you suspected."

"I was pissed."

She bit her lower lip again. God, the way she tortured that lip...

"And now?" she asked, her voice shaking just enough to have him softening. "Now that you know the truth, are you still angry at what I did?"

He lifted a shoulder. "I got over it."

Her eyes hadn't left his. "When?"

"I don't know. Soon as I realized you weren't wasting my time, I guess. When I saw that I could still get the pictures I needed."

Emma stared at him, looking shaken and...

Oh, damn.

Aroused.

She looked aroused and his body leaped to join the fray.

7

"So you really knew," Emma said. "You knew the entire time..." She shouldn't have felt so shocked. After all, she was a terrible actress, which explained why she did what she did for a living and *wrote* scripts instead of playing them out.

But she *was* shocked, to the core, and it reverberated through her body, leaving her staring at him like some dimwit.

And then there was everything else racing through her. She was cold, for one. The wind had seeped inside her. Her hair was driving her crazy because it kept sticking to her lipstick and stabbing her in the eyes, but as unbelievable as it was, her body hummed with an excitement she couldn't deny.

Maybe it was because he'd known she wasn't Amber and he'd still gone on with the shoots, which meant she'd done it. She'd given him as good as her sister would have. That was exciting in its own right.

But then there was the way he stared at her, looking frustrated and brooding, with that low, sexy voice that had said things like *Turn this way. Arch your back. Yeah, oh yeah, like that...*

God, she loved his voice. She'd tried not to think about it because she'd thought he was talking to Amber, but he hadn't been. He'd been talking to her all along.

"What I don't know is why," he said. "Why are you here pretending to be Amber?"

"She's away. But she said it was really important to her career—"

"It is. That's why I don't get it. What's keeping her away—" He shook his head. "You know what? I don't care."

"She was with a guy on the islands. I'm sorry."

"Are you kidding? I just hope he keeps her there."

That startled a laugh out of her.

"I thought you were playing me," he said.

"That's why you were mad?" When he nodded, she shook her head. "I wasn't trying to play you at all. It was for Amber. Do you have a sister?"

"Sure. Two of them. Carolyn and Tessa."

"Are you close?"

"Yes," he said. "Very. But much as I love them, I wouldn't go modeling for one of them in a thong."

She laughed. "Well, you know Amber. She gets herself into trouble."

"Yes."

"And I get her out of trouble. It's our routine."

"Ah." He nodded. "You're the oldest."

"By three whole minutes." She shook her head.

"And every time she calls and needs something, I tell myself it'll be the last time I do it, but..."

"But you can't stop—"

"Rafe."

Emma jumped at the sound of Stone's voice calling out. She'd actually forgotten they weren't the only two people on earth.

"Weather's gone," Stone said.

"We're nearly done." Rafe looked at the sky. "You guys go ahead and head back. We'll be right behind you."

"Hurry, or you'll get a nice cold shower," Stone said, and in less than two minutes, everyone and everything but Rafe, his camera and Emma had vanished.

He was changing film. "Are you too cold?"

"Define *too* cold."

He shot her a quick grin and it nearly paralyzed her with its potency. "You look almost human when you do that," she said.

"Do what?"

"Smile."

He straightened away from the camera. "I smile a lot."

"Not around me you don't."

"You mean not around you being Amber."

"Ah." She nodded, then jerked in surprise when an icy snowflake landed on her arm. "It's...snowing."

He tilted his head back, eyed the clouds, then smiled

again. "Yeah. Amazing, isn't it? We're only a couple of hours from Los Angeles, and—"

"And it's a different world."

Again their eyes locked and this time it was her heart that jerked. What was it about him that did that to her? Another snowflake landed on her shoulder and nearly sizzled off her skin. "Rafe… What is it you're looking for?"

"Peace. Quiet. Enough hours in the day to do whatever I want. Not to have to deal with Hollywood ever again."

She smiled. "I meant right now. What is it you're looking for right now, so that we can finish."

"Oh." He actually seemed a little embarrassed.

"It's just that I thought you were in a hurry," she said when he bent to his camera.

"I wanted to beat the weather. We've done that." He peeked at her. "Are you tired?"

"All I've done is stand here."

"Amber would be."

"I'm sure."

"Yeah? So why didn't you act like Amber when you were imitating her?"

"I can do that now, if you'd like."

He smiled again. "No, thanks. I'm almost done. I just wanted to try… Turn toward me so that you're fully facing the camera. See what we get that way—Yeah. Now, hands to your side so you don't cover the body or clothing. We're getting a clothing allowance here—God forbid you cover it or they'll cut my budget. Nice."

She'd placed her back to the rock, laid her arms alongside her body and leaned her head back to see if she could catch any more snowflakes. His low, husky voice made her shiver.

"Perfect," he said softly, and started taking more pictures, though he was quieter than he had been before.

Because he'd opened up without meaning to? Probably. And something deep within her wanted to put them on a level playing field. "Peace and quiet is my thing, too," she said.

"Uh-huh. I imagine working for a soap opera that needs to put out an hour of production on a daily basis is real quiet."

"Well…" She had to laugh. "I can pretend."

"You love what you do?"

She watched the sky churn and burn. "I love what I do."

"Press your shoulders to the rock. Bend a knee."

As another flake hit her bared belly, she did as he asked. For the next few moments they were photographer and model, nothing more. Up until now, it had been like a fantasy. She had played at being Amber, played at being able to model, but now that cover was gone.

She wasn't Amber, she was herself.

Just herself.

Just Emma.

Not sexy, not open and wild, not anything this man expected. But then, that was the thing about expectations...they could change.

She hoped.

At the touch of hands on her arms, she jumped.

"Just me." Rafe had stopped taking pictures and had come close. "You're cold," he said, and when she shivered—not because she was cold, but because he spoke near her ear and it sent a wave of something hot and hungry down her spine—he glided his hands up and down her arms. "I have everything I need, let's go."

But he was still touching her. His hands were on her arms. His body had leaned in, so that she felt the hard rock at her back and his hard body at her side. He'd done it in a gesture meant to warm, but it was doing something else entirely.

"Rafe—"

"You've got goose bumps bigger than the snowflakes." He pulled his sweater over his head, leaving him in a plain dark blue T-shirt, and offered the sweater to her. "Here."

She stared at it. "This would make interesting pages. Hero offers sweater to the woman who's not who she said she was."

"Is work always on your mind?"

"Yes," she said honestly, while he tugged his sweater over her head. The inside still held his body heat, his scent and she hugged her arms to herself to keep it close. The arms of the sweater went past the tips of her fingers and when he pulled the body of it down her torso, his fingers brushed her sides, her hips, her thighs where the bottom of the sweater hit.

Yes, work always had been on her mind.

Up until now, that is.

But she didn't say that, didn't feel like exposing herself to him any further. By the time he stepped back just a little, his hands still on her waist, her body tingled from head to toe and it had nothing, nothing at all, to do with the weather.

"Thank you."

"You're quite welcome."

His fingers squeezed just a little, making her realize something else. He was touching her for the first time, not as her photographer, but as a man.

And yet she was smart enough to know this wasn't reality. Reality was home with her laptop frantically trying to get her pages done. Reality was being yelled at by a shortsighted studio executive who wanted bland, stupid characters.

She had to admit, though, that the scenery out here was damn inspiring. She should reassess that whole home-office thing—

"What are you thinking?" he asked quietly.

"That if I had my laptop right this minute I could do my pages in a third of the time I usually take."

He blinked, then slowly shook his head. Finally, he

let out a little laugh and scratched his head. "You're still thinking about work."

"Aren't you?"

He just looked at her for a moment, and her heart took yet another leap.

She wasn't even sure the poor organ could take it. "Rafe—" She let out a laugh that sounded nervous even to her ears. "If you're waiting for the kiss you told me Amber gave you every time you worked together—"

"I made that up."

"Why?"

"I wanted to shake you up."

Now her laugh sounded just plain shaky. "Well, you did that, all right. You shook me up so much I couldn't think of anything else."

"I didn't think I would be sorry for telling you that lie, but I am."

"I'm…not holding a grudge."

"I'm glad—"

Then, in a move that shocked her, he invaded her space—he had quite a habit of doing that and, she had to admit, she liked it. He spread both hands wide on her back, pulled her close, stared down into her eyes and covered her mouth with his.

Hot, wet and deliciously deep for one beat, he pulled away all too quickly, then stepped back so that his hands fell away from her. "There. Now we're even."

''Right.'' With little to no encouragement, she would have asked him for another. Hell, she might even have begged.

But he'd already turned away.

Interlude over.

Which was a good thing. Back to that reality she'd so conveniently forgotten about.

For both of them.

8

RAFE AND STONE SAT in Rafe's backyard, at the patio table, looking at the proofs they'd spread out in front of them. January through April.

January and February with Amber were good, taken before she'd gone off to who-knows-where with who-knows-whom. They would fit into the calendar as planned.

Then there was March. Emma in Kauai in that sheer white number, her lush body surrounded by lush forest in a way that would make a grown man drool.

Rafe sure as hell was drooling.

Then there was April, and the desert shots. In that so-called hiking outfit she'd defined the word *sexy*. He looked at the very last shot he'd taken that day, where there'd been just a hint of a come-hither smile. He'd caught her just before she'd opened her mouth to nab a snowflake on her tongue.

Her innocent senusualness had driven him to dream about her all week. It was hard to concentrate on getting his new life in order, including finding some nice women to date, when all he could think of was Emma.

Not that she wasn't nice, but she was not what he

was looking for. First of all, she was in the business. The Hollywood business.

He knew it was wrong of him to judge her on that alone, but the fact remained that he knew what it did to a person. And he wanted out.

Then there were her little workaholic tendencies. Admirable that she worked so hard, but damn it, he'd worked hard for so many years. Now that he planned on cutting back, he wanted a woman he could actually *see* on a regular basis. Wanted someone who could and would give her all to *both* her job and a relationship.

Thinking that he might be judging her unfairly, he'd actually tried to contact her to talk. She hadn't been available and hadn't returned his call.

Not exactly a good sign.

"What do you think?" Stone asked.

"Not bad."

Stone laughed softly. "Not bad, my ass. Those shots in Kauai, and especially those in the desert—they're the best ones I've seen you do, and I've seen you do plenty."

"The ones of Amber aren't bad, either."

"Nope, but Emma is better." Stone grinned. "You don't think Amber would be pissed to see these side by side? She's going to know, too, though don't count on her admitting it."

Amber would know; she had an eye for such things.

"Are we set for the next shot?" Stone asked. "Local, right?"

"Poolside." Rafe looked around him. "Right here, as a matter of fact."

Stone nodded. "I could use a week off from traveling."

So could Rafe. The cat that had been asleep in his lap lifted its head and looked around sleepily. Her brown-gray fur stuck up in spots and was missing in others. "Meow."

Stone's eyes widened. "I can't believe you kept that mangy thing."

"She kept me." Rafe looked down at the cat.

The cat stared back at Rafe, then jumped down and padded over to a set of two bowls by the steps leading inside. One had water, the other was empty. She looked back at him balefully.

"I just fed you, Puddles."

"Puddles?" Stone repeated.

Stone shrugged. "She's the color of one."

"A mud puddle, maybe."

The cat batted at the empty bowl.

Rafe sighed and looked at Stone. "She's a bottomless pit, I swear."

Stone grimaced. "She needs a bath."

"She's not exactly fond of water."

"She's not exactly the cute little puppy you'd planned on, either," Stone noted.

He grinned helplessly. "I keep showing her the door and she keeps refusing to get out."

"It's a cat," Stone said. "You put your foot to its butt and push."

He'd thought about it, especially that first night when she'd demanded to go out at three in the morning. He'd just fallen asleep when she'd started in again, from the outside this time, wanting back in. They'd had a little discussion that night, and ever since, she'd been more considerate about her hours.

And he couldn't resist opening his door to her when she asked to come in.

Stone tapped his fingers on the pictures. "Forget the cat. These are good. Damn good. We're well on our way to a great project. I think we can finish the entire fantasy calendar in the scheduled time."

"Depends on the model situation."

"You mean, if Amber comes back and pulls her usual shit on us?" Stone shook his head. "Maybe you'll get smart and keep the *right* woman working for us."

Rafe laughed mirthlessly. "The right woman?"

"Okay, maybe not necessarily the right one, but definitely the easy one. *Emma.*" Stone skimmed his gaze over the pictures again and let out a low whistle. "Man, she is something. You are going to go for it, right?"

"Why?"

Stone cocked a brow. "Because if you don't... maybe I will."

Rafe tried to decide why that bugged him so much. "Why?"

Stone laughed. "Because she's nice on the eyes. Because she can hold a conversation and doesn't appear to be chemically dependent. Do you have any idea how rare that combination is in our business?"

Yes, damn it. He did. He tried to shrug it off, say to Stone, *What the hell, do whatever you want.* But the words wouldn't come.

"You going to tell me to back off or not?" Stone asked.

"Not." But he ground his back teeth together at the look of glee on Stone's face. "Okay, wait. Back off."

"You hate models. You hate seeing people within the business. You hate—"

"She's not a model. And she's only sort of in the business."

"She's a writer, for God's sake. That's even worse, Rafe. They work all night, they talk to themselves and they're all a little nuts."

"Then, you won't mind leaving her the hell alone," Rafe said, refusing to acknowledge Stone's laugh. He stared at the damn cat, who'd hopped off his lap and was busy sniffing around the wildflowers on the outskirts of his lawn. He tried to focus on the mangy thing, but all he could see was Stone's annoying grin. "What is so damn funny?"

"You like her."

"What is this, high school?"

"You *really* like her."

"We need to pick one of those pics for April."

"Admit it," Stone said.

"Stone?"

He was still grinning. "Yeah?"

"Shut up."

JUST AS KAUAI HAD, Joshua Tree threw Emma off.

Normally, her life was a series of routines. Up at six, she would shower, grab a bagel and either head into the studio for meetings or sit at home and write.

And write. Stopping only for scheduled breaks to feed herself and tend to business.

Lately, though, she'd been doing this with one eye on the page count, forcing herself to finish just one more page before she could get up and check e-mail. Just one more page before she could check the weather channel for the heck of it.

Apparently, she'd become afflicted with a serious attention deficit disorder. Because of her newfound tendency to leap on any diversion, all phones were pointedly ignored until lunchtime when, over a cup of noodle soup, she'd return the necessary calls.

And ignore any others, such as those from her mother.

After lunch, she had to exert tremendous discipline to sit and write, not getting up until it was time for dinner—whatever frozen dinner she had in her freezer—and watching *E!, That's Hollywood* or some other gossipy celebrity show to which she had a secret addiction.

Before her stint as a model, she would usually write some more after dinner, until her eyes closed right there in her chair, and exhausted, she'd drop into bed. Now, more often than not, Emma simply stared at the blinking cursor, her thoughts shifting from plot problems in her script to how incredibly sexy she had felt posing for Rafe, knowing that he had watched her. Not Amber, but her. Funny how for most of the day she could keep the erotic thoughts at bay—or at the very least channel them into some steamy dialogue and even steamier actions for her characters.

But when night came, she only saw Rafe, intense and demanding, staring at her, wearing next to nothing, through the lens of his camera.

Emma wondered what her mother would think of the fact that she'd impersonated Amber on a photo shoot in less clothing than one might see in a *Playboy* ad…

And that Emma had liked it…

And was secretly hoping to do it again…

Would her mother still prefer Emma over Amber? Or would she think Emma had forsaken her brains for beauty and give up on her, too? For the first time she could remember, Emma didn't care what her mother thought. She just wanted to feel that sexy, that sensual, again. She wanted Rafe's hot gaze traveling all over her....

Lord, it was official, she'd lost her mind. She'd gone off her routine; she'd gone off the deep end.

She wanted to pose again. More than she wanted to work.

Which was why she hadn't called Rafe back. She'd be crazy to do it again. Crazy.

So when the phone rang and her caller ID said "R. Delacantro," her heart nearly stopped. But her finger hit the on button before she could prevent herself. "Hello," she said, trying to sound normal when her heart was now beating so loudly, he surely could hear it.

He paused. "Emma."

"Yes."

He let out a breath. "Thought so."

Only her mother had ever been able to tell them apart on the telephone. That had led to some interesting escapades when they were children, and even more when they'd been teens. Girlfriends, boyfriends, teachers...they'd fooled everyone.

"Were you trying to reach Amber?"

"Yes," he said.

Oh. That deflated her a bit. "She's—"

"No, wait." He blew out a breath. "Hell. I called a few days ago."

"I...know. To talk to Amber?"

"I've learned to personally call her before a job,"

he said. ''To make sure she's going to be there on time. It's poolside, you got the memo?''

So he hadn't called for her. ''Yes.''

''I have no idea which of you is coming tomorrow...''

''Amber promised to be there.''

''Ah.''

The tension that was always between them, the tension she knew was purely sexual—at least on her part—shimmered so thickly she could hardly breathe. She waited for him to say something, anything.

Why don't you come instead, Emma would be nice.

Or *It'd be nice to see you again.*

But he didn't say either.

And she didn't say anything.

And after she'd hung up, she stared blindly at her computer for several moments.

Then she picked up the phone and called Amber. While it rang, she practiced her speech.

You've got to come back.

I'm swamped at work and can't help you anymore.

Your photographer is doing things to my insides and I can't take it.

''Hello?'' Amber said, sounding just a little breathless, as if she'd run to find the phone.

Or as if she was busy being seduced by Ricardo.

''Amber.'' Emma squeezed her eyes shut and tried to remember the speech. *You've got to come back. I'm swamped at work and can't help you anymore.*

Your photographer is doing things to my insides and I can't take it.

Simple.

"You've got a shoot tomorrow," she heard herself say. "Poolside. Need me to handle it for you?"

9

"OH MY GOD," Amber cried. "Emma, you are the best sister ever! I've been trying to figure out how to call you and ask, but I didn't know how. You wouldn't mind, really?"

Emma thunked her head down on her desk. What the hell was wrong with her? How hard would it have been to say what she'd rehearsed?

And why had her brain refused to say it, instead offering to traipse over to Rafe's house and put on a little bikini and let herself go through the agony of another shoot?

"No," she said a little too fast. "I wouldn't mind. Amber...do you really call me Queen Emma behind my back?"

Amber laughed. "Well, you have to admit, it suits you."

"How so?" she asked indignantly.

"So serious, so anal— And I mean that in the most loving way. Seriously, Emma. It's a compliment. And I'm so glad you're willing to hang in there with Rafe. You're such a good sport! Kenny and I are really having a time here."

"I thought his name was Ricardo."

"Oh! Well...I met Kenny a few days ago and..."

Forehead still on her desk, Emma shook her head while her sister rambled on about why she'd ditched Ricardo and how "yummy" Kenny was.

"I'm sure I'll be home by the following shoot," Amber finally said, whispering now. "Besides, my agent's been calling. I have a few TV auditions lined up—can you believe it?"

"Why are you whispering?"

"Because Kenny wants to break into modeling and no one is biting. He's depressed. I don't want him to hear how successful I am."

Emma kept her eyes closed. "That's very sweet of you."

"I know. If he knew how amazing this calendar of me was going to be, he'd be green with jealousy."

Amber's calendar.

Not Emma's, though after tomorrow she'd have done more of it than Amber had. She sighed. "I've got to go. I've got work."

"Like always."

Emma ignored that because...well, because it was true. She always had work. Without it, she was... Actually, she'd worked so long and so hard, she had no idea who she was without it.

She thought about that for the rest of the night as she worked like mad so that she could take the next day off without worrying about it.

Then she woke up at the crack of dawn to work some more.

Or more correctly, to stare at a blank screen some more. Kauai and Joshua Tree had given her great inspiration, and she'd indeed enjoyed taking her characters into uncharted territory.

Sexy and wild territory.

The problem was, she'd used her recent experiences to build up the sexual tension, but now it was time to…consummate. She'd written love scenes before, plenty of times. She'd even had her own sexual relationships but they'd always lacked something. All the candles and soft music in the world couldn't make a love scene work if the chemistry wasn't there.

And she knew little about chemistry. Or she had known little, until the past few weeks when she'd gotten quite the lesson.

She had more to learn, a lot more. Could she go today and somehow get Rafe to show her the rest? And did she really think she could handle the rest, and then walk away?

Because she *would* walk away, she would have to. It wasn't that she didn't want a man in her life—she just didn't know what to do with one. Or how to hang on to one. Sure, she could turn heads, but that was exterior stuff. She'd never be able to keep a man like Rafe satisfied for long.

But she didn't need long. She only needed a day.

An hour.

Her body tingled at the thought. When it was time, she rose from her chair and grabbed the directions to the day's shoot.

Her knees knocked together as she headed over there. They would have sent a car for her, but she wanted her own car there so she could leave when she was ready.

Her mode of escape.

Rafe lived in the Glendale Hills above LA. After following a series of long, winding streets, she came out on a cul-de-sac with stunning views of the city.

His house was on the end, a Tudor-cottage style, cream with dark blue wood trim and shutters. The yard had a green lawn that needed mowing and was lined with wildflowers that had taken over all the tree beds, as well. It was large but homey, and she liked the way the gardens didn't have a manicured look to them. She'd bet if Rafe didn't take care of this place, no one did, and she found herself trying to picture him out here on his days off. He'd be shirtless, of course—

''Meow.''

Before she could knock on the door, a cat appeared out of nowhere. A small, scrawny brown-and-gray cat with odd tufts of fur sticking up here and there. ''Hello,'' she said softly, and reached out to pet it.

The cat went very still, as if not quite sure if he—or she—was going to allow the touch, but once Emma scratched beneath its chin, it came a little closer. Emma knocked on the front door, then squatted to pet the cat, who was now rubbing against her ankles, eager for more chin scratching.

The door opened, and high above her stood Rafe. As in her earlier fantasy, he was shirtless, wearing only a pair of khaki cargo shorts, and she felt her mouth fall open because up close he was even better than any fantasy.

Research, she reminded herself. *You're here for the research.*

And fun. Let it begin.

He propped a shoulder against the doorjamb and eyed her. "Emma."

"Yes."

He let out a breath, apparently unsure if Emma being the model for the day, was a good or bad thing. "You didn't get the message, I take it."

"Message?"

"The shoot is at four o'clock instead of one. Is that cat...purring?"

They both stared down at the feline, whose eyes were half-closed, face slack with pleasure as Emma continued to scratch it beneath the chin. A rusty, sporadic rumble sounded from its throat.

"I think so." Emma smiled. "Is it yours?"

"No, but I think I'm hers." Rafe pushed away from the doorjamb and hunkered down before the cat, which brought all the broad expanse of bare, tanned, sinewy flesh far too close to Emma for comfort. He smelled like fresh air and soap and male.

"She showed up on my doorstep a few weeks ago and hasn't left since." Rafe seemed baffled by this as he reached out to scratch the cat's back. "I don't want to hurt her feelings, but I was hoping to get a puppy after this last shoot is over and I can't exactly do that with her hanging around."

He wanted a puppy. Why did that make her want to melt into a boneless heap on the floor?

Ecstatic at his touch, the cat did as Emma had nearly done—fell to the ground with a loud "oomph" and exposed her belly.

With a soft laugh, Rafe stroked her, laughing again when the purring got louder.

As for Emma, she couldn't laugh, she could hardly breathe. It seemed so juvenile, but she couldn't tear her eyes off his bare chest, which was hard, tough and oh-so-touchable. And then there was his six-pack stomach and, man oh man, she wished he'd do as the cat had and lay down so she could stroke him.

Embarrassed at the thought, she covered her mouth as if she'd spoken out loud. She stared at him.

"What?" he asked.

"Nothing."

Giving her a funny look, he rose and put out a hand to pull her up, as well. At the connection of their fingers, she'd have sworn she felt a jolt to her toes.

"'Nothing' doesn't make you slap a hand over your mouth," he noted.

"It's because I have a habit of thinking out loud,"

she said through her fingers. "It's the hazard of working alone—you start talking to yourself."

"Ah." He eyed her. "Were your thoughts that bad?"

"Um." She bit her fingers. "Define 'bad.'"

"'Bad' as in...I don't know. You're here against your will, you can't stand the sight of me, you can't wait until we're done... Pick one."

Slowly she shook her head. "I'm not here against my will," she said. "And I can stand the sight of you, fairly easily, actually. That's the problem."

"Problem?"

"You're...different today."

"I'm not feeling the need to kill your sister for a change."

"Oh." She smiled.

And so did he. "I guess for the first time you're seeing the real me."

She liked the real him, too much not to be honest. "You should know, I came for the research."

His gaze met hers, dark, hot. "Research?"

"I need inspiration for...a particular storyline. I thought modeling for you could help. And it has."

"Really."

"Yes." She closed her eyes. "Because when I go home afterwards I'm...in an inspired sort of mood."

"Could you define 'inspired sort of mood'?"

"Hot."

"Hot," he repeated in a funny voice, but she didn't dare look.

"Yes," she said. "And bothered." *Let's not forget that.* "I've written the best storylines ever in the past few weeks, and all because of working with you." She opened her eyes. A mistake that, as she found herself looking at two perfectly formed pecs lightly dusted with dark hair.

"Emma," he said, still with that tight voice.

"Yeah?"

He slid his fingers to her jaw and lifted her gaze to his, which was filled with that heat and also a good amount of reluctant humor.

"I need to stop you right now and tell you. I have this thing against being attracted to women in my business world."

"I'm only pretending to be in your business world."

"You're a writer. A Hollywood soap opera writer who lives for her work."

"What does that have to do with my research on...hot stuff?"

"Is that all this is?" he asked softly, his hand still on her face, his broad shoulders blocking her view of anything but him. "Research?"

"What else could it be?" She felt breathless, because there was no denying what a small part of her wanted to hear. As crazy as it sounded, she wanted him to say these sensations meant far more than research.

His finger stroked her jawline all the way to her ear, which he slowly rimmed, drawing a shudder from her.

"I have no idea what else it could be, but I do know one thing. I want to touch you. I never want to touch my models, but I want to touch you."

"Maybe it's because I'm not really your model." His eyes met hers. "You know I'm not."

"But you are for today." He sighed. "Hell. Look, let's just get this shoot done. I have the bathing suit and all the gear."

"But I'm too early. What about the crew?"

"I think we know what we're doing by now, don't you?"

Well, she knew *he* knew what he was doing. Her body was still pulsing from just a light touch to her ear. But as for her, no. She had no idea what she was doing.

"Come on, Emma," he said silkily. "Let's do this. All in the name of your…research."

Right. All in the name of research.

10

RAFE LED EMMA through his house. He'd gotten used to the mostly bare rooms that were waiting for him to make them his own. He wondered what she would think.

Emma was quiet as they walked through the empty living room, but when they passed the equally empty dining room, she said, "You do live here, right?"

"Yeah, I know, it's hard to tell. That's going to change after this calendar."

"Why?"

"I'm getting off the circuit."

"You're retiring?"

"From Hollywood, yes." He took her down a hallway, stark except for a stack of framed pictures leaning against the walls that he'd taken over the years but hadn't yet hung.

When they got to the den, she smiled. "Ah. I can see you've claimed one room, at least."

She was right. Here, in the large room with the high, opened-beamed ceiling, he had a big-screen TV and sound system against one wall and the largest sectional couch on the market against the other—one on which he could make his six-foot-two-inch frame comfortable.

The other two walls were all windows, looking out his backyard and pool, which he'd hosed down and cleaned earlier in anticipation of this shoot. The previous owner had grown a lush garden of wildflowers and trees bordering the grass, with brick paths and stone benches surrounded by pots of more flowers.

"It's beautiful," she said, going to the glass. "I can see why you wanted to shoot here."

"The calendar calls for a pool shot." He walked up behind her and took in the same view. "I figured, why not here." Her hair tickled his nose and the scent of her filled his senses. He knew he was tempting fate to do this without a crew, but he had wanted to see what would happen, if, after a couple of weeks of this teasing, he'd still feel attracted.

He did. "Are you ready to do this?"

When she nodded, he retrieved the Nordstrom bag he'd had on a kitchen table.

She swallowed. "The costume?"

"The costume," he confirmed, and reached into the bag.

When he dangled the black crocheted bikini from his fingers, she swallowed again but took it from him, her fingers entangling with his for one brief moment.

Holding on, he squeezed hers. "When you look at me like that, you drive me crazy."

"Look at you like…what?"

Vulnerable and unsure, yet sexy as hell. He just shook his head. ‘‘You realize you could just walk away. This is Amber’s problem, not yours.’’

‘‘Where should I change?’’

‘‘Emma—’’

‘‘I’m doing this, Rafe. I promised I would, and—’’

‘‘And…?’’

‘‘And I want to.’’

He stared at her for a long moment, then shrugged. After all, he didn’t want her to back out. He showed her to the bathroom and then went outside with his camera, not wanting to think about what he had to do, which was look at her in a bikini for at least an hour.

He tinkered with his equipment, setting up near the edge of the pool, with the hills in the background. There was a metallic silver float drifting on the water. He wanted her there, face down, hands together beneath her chin, legs slightly apart, drifting away from him. He’d pictured it long before he’d ever met Emma, knowing how perfect, how mouthwatering the shot would be.

What he hadn’t known was how exciting Emma would be, personally. He had the camera on the tripod and was playing with his settings when he heard the sliding glass door open behind him.

His pulse tripled but he kept his concentration on the camera, telling himself this was ridiculous, he’d taken hundreds, *thousands* of shots of supermodels across the globe, and not one of them had ever moved him personally.

There was a light breeze, which maybe would cool him off. His hair lifted from his damp forehead as the water slapped against the tiles.

Just another regular day of work.

He heard the pad of her bare feet as she came close, and with a little grimace, he lifted his head.

Any cooling effects from the breeze vanished.

The black crocheted bikini fit her as if it'd been made for her, lovingly cupping her full breasts, between her thighs, the yarn stretching, giving him peekaboo hints of creamy skin beneath.

She stopped about five feet away. Too far to touch her or smell her. Too far to see the pulse at the base of her neck, to judge if she was as affected as he.

But the puckered tips of her nipples, almost but not quite poking through the black string of her top, told him the truth.

Even as it nearly killed him.

He knew from that day in Kauai, when she'd worn nothing more than damp white silk, exactly how gorgeous she was; how full and high her breasts were even without support; how the color of her nipples was that of a perfect rosebud. When those nipples were aroused, as they were now, they made his knees weak.

Just standing there looking at her, he felt his body tighten. Painfully so.

He also knew from that day on that lush, wet island,

when she'd worn nothing but a tiny strip of a thong, that she'd had to have either shaved or waxed her bikini line. He pictured her doing that this morning in preparation for this shoot, but the thought nearly undid him and his cargo shorts became a torture chamber.

Was she as wet as he was hard? If he tugged those bottoms loose from her body, preferably with his teeth, would he see just how wet?

"How's this?" she asked, sounding just breathless enough to make him want to groan.

"Good." His voice came out hoarse so he cleared his throat. "Damn good. So good I'm not sure I'll remember how to use the camera."

She put a hand to her belly as if nervous. "You probably say that to all your models."

He shook his head.

"No?"

"No."

"Never?"

"Never. I've never had any trouble concentrating on a shoot before," he told her. "But I'm having trouble now."

She dragged her bottom lip across her teeth. "It's probably wrong to admit this, but seeing as we're being so open…I like that you're having trouble." Her breathing wasn't close to steady. "I should be taking notes, writing down all my jumbling emotions and body's reactions to you for my research, but honestly, I can't think clearly enough for that."

Research. Right. Grateful for the reminder that she was here for that, he pointed to the metallic float. "That's the prop."

"What about makeup?"

"You're going to be facing away from the camera." He tossed her a bottle of baby oil. "Slick up first so the water will bead off you."

Eyes on his, she opened the bottle and squirted the oil onto her palm. Slowly she began to spread it onto her skin—her legs, her arms, her belly, her chest, her back.

"Hair?" she whispered, straightening.

"Wet. All of you needs to be wet." He had to look away from her when her pupils dilated. "Just slick your hair back from your face when you get in the pool."

Turning away from him, she waded in, sucking in a breath as the cool water lapped at her calves, her thighs…between them. Craning her neck, she kept her eyes on his as she sank in a little deeper, to her breasts, and then ducked entirely under.

He let out a shaky breath.

When she surfaced, she slicked back her hair and reached for the float.

"On your stomach," he said.

She pulled herself up until she was lying flat on her belly. Water sluiced off her, running in little rivulets down her slim spine, off her long legs. Between them.

His mouth went dry. ''Arms bent a little, so that your hands, fingers flexed, float on top of the water.''

Following his directions to the letter, she did as he asked.

''Eyes closed,'' he instructed. ''Lie on one cheek, chin up slightly, hair to one side.''

She was now sprawled out, water beading on her, looking like a goddess. He let out a slow breath. ''Spread your legs a little.''

She went utterly still, then slowly, very slowly, spread her legs an inch or two.

''More.''

This time she didn't hesitate, digging her toes into opposite corners of the float. The picture of her lying there, body offered up, wet and shiny, arms and legs spread, had him staring, mesmerized.

''Rafe?''

Blinking, he put his eye to the lens and sucked in another breath. ''Yeah. Perfect.'' He took a few shots, his body tight as an arrow. ''Are you thinking about your research?''

''I told you, I...I can't.''

''Because of the jumbling emotions and your body's reactions.''

''Yes.''

He kept snapping the shutter. ''What are they? The jumbling emotions.''

She turned her head and glanced at him with a question in her eyes.

He managed a smile. "Maybe I can remind you later, when you're trying to write it all down."

"Oh." She lay her head down again. "Mmm, the water feels nice. That's my first emotion—pleasure. Then there's the power."

"Power?"

"Yes."

Since her head was turned to the side, he could see only half her face. Her mouth curved slightly, and it was so feminine, so wily and sure that he felt it all the way to his toes, but he kept taking pictures.

"When you talk to me in your professional mode," she said softly, "when you're being The Photographer, your voice is cool, calm. Even."

"Is it?"

"Oh, yes. But sometimes, like now, you talk to me in that low, throaty voice that tells me you're not thinking cool and calm. You're not thinking work. You're thinking…"

"What?"

"Sex," she said. "You're thinking about sex, and I made you think about it. That's the power. I mean *I* did that to you. *I* made you lose your concentration. You know what else?"

He was afraid to know, truly he was. But he stepped away from the camera and walked around the edge of the pool so he could see her face more clearly. "What?"

Her slight smile turned to a full-fledged grin. "I like it."

His body tightened even more. "You like that you're driving me right off the edge of control?"

"Yes." She dipped her fingers in the water and played a little. Splashed him. "But to be honest, I'm also embarrassed."

"Are you kidding?" He moved back behind his camera. He was safer there. "Why?"

"Because of the view you've got." She wiggled, just a little. "I know the bathing suit is riding up, and with the angle you're at, I'm wondering what you can see."

"What I can see..." He took a good long look at her long legs, at the juncture of her thighs, how the black crocheted bottoms outlined her so perfectly. Then she squirmed slightly, and he nearly moaned at the sight. "I can see that you have the most heart-stopping legs on the planet. Your slim back is arched slightly, and the low-riding bikini exposes your butt enough that I can see your adorable twin dimples just above the top of the material."

"I just had another jumbling emotion," she said softly.

"Really? Tell me."

"This is...turning me on," she whispered.

She said the words in a way that made them seem like a conspirator's secret, and his knees went shaky. "That's reaction, not emotion. And it's not very specific, not as far as your writing goes.'' He had no idea why he was doing this, teasing them both into a fiery lather, but he couldn't stop now. ''Be specific, Emma.''

Her eyes were still shut, and he clicked away as she searched for the words or courage to tell him. ''My skin feels too tight,'' she finally said.

''Good.'' He knew the feeling. He took his camera off the tripod and moved back to the side of the pool where he could get a better view of her face tipped toward the sun, eyes closed, the glow of excitement on her cheeks. ''More.''

''My heart is pounding like I just ran a marathon.''

He pulled his face away from the lens, stared at her. Suddenly, he couldn't do it any longer, he couldn't treat her as a model. He'd never talked to a model like this.

He wanted to treat her as a woman.

For the first time in his career, he set the camera down in the middle of a shoot. He stepped onto the first step of the shallow end of the pool, letting his feet soak up the cool water in hopes it might cool off his overheated engines.

''What else?'' he asked hoarsely.

''My nipples...they're hard and throbbing.''

He understood hard and throbbing.

She opened her eyes ''You're...done?''

''I'm done. Emma, this isn't the usual photo shoot.''

He let out a long, shuddering breath. "I've never made it personal before, but this feels pretty personal."

"What makes it different?"

"I'm not sure."

"Maybe it's because it's your last job. Or..."

"Or?"

"Maybe you were thinking you could get something out of it."

"No. God, no." He watched her shoulders relax marginally at his emphatic answer. "It's you."

She looked at him for a moment, then dumped herself into the water. She swam toward him, beneath the water, breaking the surface just in front of him. Eyes never leaving his, she started up the steps, the water sluicing off her as her body was revealed, inch by glorious wet inch.

Drawn to her as if they were bound together, he took the next step down, meeting her halfway, and then suddenly they were lunging at each other, hands grappling for purchase, mouths mating, bodies straining while the water splashed around them.

He never even felt the water soaking into his shorts, nor the sun beating down on his back. All he felt was her body coming alive beneath his hands.

His certainly did.

Research, my ass, he thought, one hand skimming up her slim spine, the other cupping her butt in his hand, squeezing just a little, loving the feel of her hot skin and the cool water running down it. She felt so good against him, he would have liked to keep her there for days, until he had lapped her up from head to toe and felt sated.

More than anything, he wanted to have the time to do that, right here, right now.

As for the kiss, it was their first real one. He didn't count Kauai or the desert. Those had been nice, sweet even, but each nothing more than a quick contact, a tease, a moment of playfulness.

Not this kiss.

This kiss stabbed him deep in the belly with its sharp, needy claws, and had nothing to do with quick or playful. This kiss was the result of weeks of hunger and desire. And though he had never been told of her past, of her sexual experiences, when he opened his mouth and slid his tongue in to dance with hers, he knew.

When she gripped him tighter and let out a soft gasp, he knew.

This wasn't just two people scratching an itch, this wasn't research, or a job, no matter what they claimed.

This was just two people, a man and a woman, looking for that elusive thing only a few lucky bastards ever really found.

Looking to be loved.

11

WHEN THEY BROKE APART FOR AIR, Emma gulped in a few breaths and stared at him. She could hear him panting, too, could see him staring at her, as if he wasn't sure how she'd gotten into his arms.

During the past crazy few minutes, she hadn't even noticed, but they'd stumbled down yet another step and now stood thigh deep in his pool, skin to skin except for his drenched shorts and her skimpy bikini. It was difficult to look at him knowing that the kiss wasn't the end to an incredibly erotic experience, but just the beginning.

Her body was shaking, close to the sort of pleasure she usually only dreamed about. She had a hard time understanding how in the past she'd had to strive so hard to climax, and yet all he'd done was kiss her and she was on the edge.

"Rafe—"

He lowered his head and kissed her again, a slow, deep, wet kiss, before slowly pulling back. "Stop me, Emma. Stop me now."

No. No way. She took in the tic in his rigidly held jaw, the pulse at his temple, the way his fingers dug into her. He wanted her. He wanted her more than she could remember being wanted. No way was she going to stop him now. She slid her fingers into the hair at the nape of his neck and tugged, trying to bring his mouth back to hers. At the same time, she practically crawled up his body, wrapping one leg around his hip, opening herself up so that she could slide against him.

This wrenched a rough groan from his throat, but he held her off, moving his hands to her hips. "Emma, if I kiss you again, we aren't going to stop there. If I kiss you again, I want you naked, beneath me, gasping my name as you come."

Her knees liquefied. "How do you know I'll... come?"

"Oh, baby, you'll come."

That cocky statement should have irritated the hell out of her; instead she ached for him to prove it. So she pulled him in for another kiss, fisting her hands in his hair to hold his head, but he didn't try to get away. One hand moved back to her bottom, the other moved to the string ties of her bikini at the back of her neck. He tugged at the knot until she felt the bow give.

He drew back slightly so that the cups of her top loosened, threatening to expose her breasts, but not quite. He picked up the very end of one string and dragged it along her collarbone, nudging the material away from her skin as he skimmed the string down the line of her cleavage. Then both his hands drew the cups down, spilling her free, exposing her to the opposing sensations of the cool water dripping from her hair and the warm spring day.

His gaze was locked on hers, and the heat and hunger there made her shudder.

"You said you wanted hot and wild," he said.

"For my research."

"We both know this isn't about your research." He dropped the strings of her top and covered her breasts with his hands.

"It...isn't?" she managed to say.

"No." He replaced his hands with his mouth.

Her legs weren't going to hold her and she heard a horrifyingly needy whimper—her own.

"Yeah. Love that sound."

Her nipples had been hard from the moment he'd answered his door shirtless, but they pebbled even more now as he teased first one and then the other with his tongue, his eyes burning with the knowledge that this wasn't about work but about them and what they did to each other, with the knowledge that he could make her so helpless, she could hardly speak. He showed her even more, bending her over his arm a little, looking his fill first, then using his thumb to slowly and maddeningly rasp over one wet and aching nipple while blowing his hot breath on the other.

She couldn't suppress her cry, or her shiver.

"Cold?" he whispered, and since she didn't have a voice, she could only shake her head. "No? Good." He got a good grip on the second black string of her top and pulled, all while watching her with those dark, dark eyes.

The black crochet fell away from her torso completely and hit the water. His palm skimmed down her belly and her eyes drifted shut.

"No fair hiding." His knuckles brushed over the material barely covering her mound. "Open your eyes, Emma." And he slid the very tops of his fingers just beneath the material.

Another whimper escaped her. Already her hips were moving in an age-old rhythm. She needed him, needed this so desperately she couldn't see, couldn't hear, could hardly draw air into her lungs.

He slid his fingers a little lower, gliding them through her thin strip of closely trimmed hair until they hovered right above where she needed him most.

Almost out of her mind, she gripped his wrist in her hand and tried to guide him to the right spot, clamping her thighs tight, holding him in place so that he couldn't move.

"I'm not going anywhere," he promised softly, mouth to her ear.

"I need—"

"Tell me."

His voice was soothing, his fingers were not.

"Mmm, nice." His finger stroked once over her, unerringly finding the right spot.

Her eyes flew open and she bit her lip to hold back the sounds trying to escape her throat, but he shook his head and leaned in, pulling on her lower lip with his teeth, then kissing the spot to soothe it. "Don't hold back, please don't hold back."

He wanted in, wanted all the way in. As if to prove it, he kept his hand in her bikini bottoms but stilled his finger, making her squirm and arch, urgently in quest of his touch.

"Tell me what you want," he coaxed. "Anything."

"You know what I want."

"Tell me."

She stared at him, words escaping her.

"Anything," he whispered again, and put his lips to her throat, dragging a hot kiss over her jaw to the sensitive spot beneath her ear, just as his fingers started moving again. Slowly he rimmed her opening, up one side and down the other, spreading her own wet heat as he went, easing his way and increasing her pleasure. "Anything, Emma..."

All she had to do was tell him, but she couldn't talk, she could only feel and what she was feeling so overwhelmed her that she had to blink rapidly just to keep her in focus.

"What is it? An orgasm?" He took more of her weight over his arm, licked the rim of her ear as he lightly skimmed his finger over the very center of her being, just a teasing, butterfly touch that was pure torment.

She stifled a cry and he let out a hot breath in her

ear as he gave her another stroke. "Is that it? You want me to touch you there?"

Her face against his throat, she nodded vigorously. Yes. Yes, she wanted him to touch her there. She wanted an orgasm. And she was almost there, almost—

"Tell me." He sucked the lobe of her ear into his mouth and slid one long finger deep inside her.

There was no stifling her cry this time, and the ache became unbearable, the gripping need for release so strong that it took on a life of its own. "Oh, please."

"I'll please anything."

He added another finger to the first, pressing deep into her as his teeth nibbled on her throat. In and out...in and out, until she was panting, whimpering, writhing. His thumb touched the swollen hub of nerve endings, pressing until her toes started to curl.

But then he eased away, and she let out a desperate, frustrated sob.

"Emma?"

She fisted one hand in his hair, the other over his chest, which was damp and thumping hard with the beat of his heart. "Make me come," she demanded.

He cupped her again, then circled his thumb over her hard little center. "Like this?"

"Yes!"

"I want to watch you," he whispered. "I want to hear you—" Around...and around...in exactly the right motion and pressure, as if he'd known her body for years. Her entire body stiffened as it started to happen. She couldn't believe it. He was making her come and she was letting him. She'd lost all the power, all the control, as it burst over her in a thousand points of light.

He kept touching her, whispering sweet nothings in her ear, telling her what else he wanted to do to her.

"Yes," she gasped. "Yes to all of it."

She slid her hand over his erection, so impressive behind his soaked cargo shorts. It wasn't enough. She reached inside and found smooth, hot, hard heaven.

"Emma." He caught her hand.

She looked into his eyes, saw the sudden regret, and went still. "You don't want to…?"

"Are you kidding? I want to, I'm dying to. But when it comes to being inside you, I don't want to rush."

She stared at him. "I thought we had plenty of time."

"Had. We've used it all up."

No. *No.*

"I'm afraid Stone's going to show up, and not only don't I want to rush once I get inside you, I don't want him to walk out here and see you."

"But…" She could barely breathe, much less talk. "What about you?"

"Maybe a cold shower will help."

Rafe didn't miss the telltale stiffening of her demeanor at that. Only a moment ago she'd still been panting for breath, and now, though she was still right here in his arms, she was as good as gone.

"I'm sorry—" he said.

She stood and backed away so fast she nearly slipped deeper into the pool, would have if he hadn't surged up and steadied her.

She pushed him away. Avoiding his gaze, she adjusted her bottoms and waded through the water for her top, which was floating by the raft. "We're done shooting, right?"

"Yes."

"Then, I'll be out of here."

"What's the matter?" he asked quietly. "Did I see too much of you?"

"Well, you did see quite a bit." She tried to tie on her top but her fingers were shaking.

Moving close, he took over, noting that as he did so, she covered her breasts with her hands. "A little late now, given that I've licked and sucked and tasted every inch of them."

She blushed at that, a fine shade of red rising up her neck and throat and over her cheeks.

When her bathing suit was in place, she sighed. "Rafe."

"Emma."

She stared at his chest rather than his eyes. "I'm not good at this." She glanced at the pool, then closed her eyes briefly. "I know I gave you the impression

I'm wild and free…but I'm not. I mean, yes, I wanted to…I asked you to…"

"Make you come?"

"I don't usually…"

"Ask, or come?"

"Either. Both."

He nearly laughed, but she wasn't kidding. Had she really never had an orgasm with a man before? How was that possible, as beautiful as she was, that no man had ever—

"I'm not like that—" She broke off when he cupped her jaw and lifted her face.

"Are you somehow trying to apologize for the fact that you had a climax?"

"Well, mostly I don't—"

"You *are,*" he said with an amazed laugh. "You're trying to apologize." He put his mouth to hers, kissed her until he felt her start to melt against him again, and then slowly pulled back. "Let's get one thing clear," he whispered against her mouth. "Your pleasure is my pleasure."

"But you didn't—"

"Next time." He kissed her again.

She stared at him. "Next time?"

"Oh, yeah."

EMMA DROVE HOME on autopilot, her body vibrating with the effects of what she'd let Rafe do to it. Even as she got herself on the freeway and tried to stop thinking, she continued to relive it.

His hands all over her, pulling off her top, slipping into her bottoms—

A little cry escaped her lips and she cranked up the music. But not even the rocking beat could take her mind off the fact that certain parts of her anatomy were still suffering little aftershocks of their pool adventure.

She'd let him— He'd—

Her hand darted out, slipped into her purse and found her cell phone. Watching the road, she punched in her sister's mobile number.

"Emma, I'm right in the middle of getting a tan here," Amber answered a little crankily.

"A tan," Emma said tightly. "You're getting yourself a tan while I live your life for you. Well, it's over, sis. You're on your own regarding the fantasy calendar. I don't know where or when your next shoot is because—" *Because I just came with your photographer's mouth on my breast and his fingers in—* No. Don't go there. She gulped in a deep, calming breath. "Well. Let's just say that I quit. Okay?"

"Jeez, how did you get your panties all in a twist?"

It hadn't been panties, thank you very much, but a bathing suit, and it had gotten twisted by Rafe's most amazing, talented fingers.

But that was another story entirely. "Look, it doesn't matter—"

"Rafe pull his cool, distant routine on you again? Oh, honey, don't take it personally. He doesn't really have a thing for models, you know? If he had his way, he'd be out taking pictures of...I don't know. *Stuff.* Not people, I don't think. So if he's all chilly and remote on you, just shrug it off."

Chilly and remote?

Ha!

That hadn't exactly been the problem.

No, the issue was her own.

Basically, her life had been easy up until now, just a series of stories she put together to give other people pleasure and to keep herself so busy that she didn't have time for anything else.

Then she'd taken one look at Rafe Delacantro on a dark, stormy Hawaiian island and everything had changed. She'd *wanted,* she'd *craved,* and she hadn't wavered from that want and craving until she'd gotten it.

And oh, how she'd gotten it.

She'd gotten hot and wild. She'd gotten the incentive she needed to spice up her storylines for the next *ten* years.

Next time.

Oh, dear God, he wanted a next time, and there'd be even more.

Her heart started a rapid tattoo just at the thought. Because the truth was, she wanted a next time, too.

12

RAFE STOOD AT THE TOP of Donner Summit Pass, the wind tossing his face and clothes, the sun at this high altitude seeming so close he could almost touch it, and drew in a deep breath. Beyond him stood the majestic Sierras, tall and craggy, lined with a carpet of towering pines and sage, dotted with the snow that unbelievably hadn't melted yet, even though it was June.

Again, he was an entire world away from Los Angeles and again he was loving it.

They'd flown up here, in an eight-seater Cessna—a "butt squeaker," Stone had called it—and had hooked up with a local who'd shown them the quickest way to get to the snow. It had involved a short hike but they'd gotten the shot they needed, with their model in a stark white zip-up leather suit, straddling a snowmobile and looking outrageously sexy.

On the flight up here, he'd ridden shotgun with the pilot, with his model in the far, far back, and because he'd been busy talking to the pilot when everyone had loaded, he hadn't gotten a good look at her.

Until they'd stepped off the plane he hadn't known who he was shooting today.

But one look into her fathomless light-brown eyes and he'd known. Emma. Emma, wanting desperately to be mistaken for Amber. The looks she shot him were filled with anxiety—that he'd reveal her, that he'd somehow refer to what they'd done in his pool—as well as a reluctant awareness.

If she thought he was going to tell anyone what had happened between them, she was sorely mistaken. He didn't want to share the details of an experience that had rocked his world.

So for the shoot he'd given her the anonymity she seemed to crave. He'd done it because he'd needed it as well, because if he acknowledged that she wasn't Amber, that she was indeed the woman he had slowly stripped and had begun to make love to, he didn't know how to be just her photographer.

But now the shoot was over and people were making their way back to the small, private Truckee/Tahoe airport where the Cessna waited to take them back to L.A.

Standing on the tarmac while everyone loaded up, Rafe maneuvered his way close to Emma. She'd changed out of the leather cat-suit that had looked amazing on her, and now wore simple black jeans and a white sweater. She'd pulled her beautiful hair back in a clip and had washed off all the makeup. She looked about sixteen. She stood with her head tilted back, soaking in the wide-open blue sky that seemed so much larger up here in the Sierras than it ever did at home.

When he touched her hand, she jumped a little and shot him a wary look.

"Emma."

She let out a long breath. "The way you do that... You know you're the only one who can tell us apart."

"It's not hard for me."

She looked at him as if she wasn't sure she liked that.

"I love the way you look in your own clothes."

Her expression went from wary to startled in a heartbeat, and then she laughed. "Yeah."

"I do."

She shook her head and looked at the mountains surrounding them, at the lovely valley just beyond the airport where wild grass shifted in the wind, making the land look alive. "After all the exquisite clothing you've been exposed to on a daily basis," she said, "you like my plain jeans and a sweater?"

"No, I like *you* in the jeans and sweater." He grinned. "Actually, I like you in nothing at all, but—"

"Shh!" She covered his mouth with her hand and looked around, but relaxed when she realized no one was paying attention to them. She turned back to his still-smiling face, and had to shake her head and let out her own smile. "I can't believe you just said that."

He pulled her hand free and kept it in his own. "I'm glad it's you here doing this."

"When did you know?"

"When I saw your face."

"After we got off the plane?"

"I tried to see you before, but you were good at keeping your face averted on the ride up here."

She looked out to the valley again, then sighed. "I don't know why that sticks with me—that you see me when no one else does."

"You're softer than Amber."

She stared at him; she slowly shook her head.

"Sweeter."

"Stop it."

"And your breathing changes when you look at me."

"No, it doesn't."

"Really?" He shifted subtly closer. Anyone looking at them would have sworn they were just having an easy conversation, heads together so that they could hear each other over the roar of the Cessna's engines starting.

But with his shoulders and body blocking Emma from view, he stroked his hand up her back, then slowly back down, applying just enough pressure that she had no choice but to take the last step between them. Her hand came up against his chest to brace herself and, in the guise of telling her something, he leaned in and nuzzled just beneath her ear.

That she let out a shaky breath, that he felt her shiver, told him everything he needed to know.

"How did the writing go last week?" he murmured. "Between the pool shoot and now?"

"I—"

When he nibbled her throat, she let out a helpless moan that reverberated through him and was the sexiest thing he'd ever heard.

"—I can't think with your mouth on me, Rafe."

He lifted his head and smiled at her, his hand still low on her back, fingers spread wide to touch as much of her as possible. "I like it when you say my name like that, just a little breathless." He stroked her again. "Tell me about the writing."

"If you believe that I can think with your hands on me, think again."

"Hey, I can't even think when you're standing right here in front of me."

That seemed to surprise her, but why, he had no idea. Did she really think she didn't affect him?

"I called you," he said.

"I know." She glanced over at the plane, where everyone had loaded but them. No one seemed to notice the two of them talking. "I wasn't sure I'd be seeing you again."

"And yet, here you are."

"Yeah." She looked into his eyes then. "Here I am." She dropped her gaze to his mouth. The wind had loosened a couple of strands of her hair, one of which clung to his jaw. He left it there, a damn good sign of how far gone over this woman he was.

"You asked me about the writing." Her eyes lit with wry humor. "The executives at the studio didn't know what to make of all the sex I put on the page. They told me to keep doing whatever it was I was doing to get inspired."

Rafe grinned, and the hand he had low on her back drifted a little lower, brushing over the very sweet curve of her butt, squeezing once before rising again. "Keeping you inspired would be my pleasure."

She looked intrigued, but also slightly wary again. "We've got to get on board," she said, eyeing the pilot talking to two men from inside the airport. He was shaking his head and consulting his clipboard, and he didn't look happy. "I think they're waiting on us."

"I have an idea."

She eyed him. "Yes, well, I have an idea what your idea is."

He laughed. "I'm capable of thinking of something other than sex."

Looking doubtful, she cocked her head and studied his expression. "I'm going to be sorry I asked, but what's your idea?"

"Stay with me here in Tahoe tonight."

"I thought this was an idea about something other than sex."

"It is. We'll find something fun to do, have a great

meal, and then go to a bed and breakfast. Fly home tomorrow, instead.''

She blinked. ''That sounds like a date. A very long one.''

With his mouth so close to her ear, he could breathe her in with every breath. He kissed her neck, felt her tremor and knew they had to follow this through. ''After everything else we've done, don't you think a date would be almost tame?''

She closed her eyes. ''I don't know...''

''You wanted hot and wild. Granted, you got a nice start on it, and I had to take cold showers all week, but there's more, so much more—'' He laughed softly when she blushed. ''Don't be shy now. Come on, Emma, aren't you in the least bit curious about the rest? I mean, we practically burn each other up just from kissing. Let's see where this goes.''

''You're talking physically.''

He knew she'd shy away from more, plus he wasn't ready to go there, either. ''Yes.''

Her gaze had drifted out to the mountains again and then she brought it back to him. ''In the name of research.''

''Does that make you feel better? To call it something other than what it is, which is an attraction, a deep one?''

She let out a huff of air but had the good grace to smile. ''I believe it does.''

''Whatever works for you, then. I just...want you.''

"Rafe—" She was still smiling, but she was going to say no, he could feel it.

But then the pilot appeared at their side, his clipboard gripped tight in his fist. "They're saying we're overloaded. They'll let on one more person, but then we're at maximum capacity."

Rafe craned his neck and looked at the plane. "How did that happen?"

"I don't know, sir. Maybe you all ate too much while you were here." He offered a feeble smile.

They must have flown up here overloaded. Rafe thought about all the small plane tragedies he'd ever heard about, and felt a little sick.

"Someone's got to stay," the pilot said apologetically. "I'll charter another flight for whoever does, or come back for them myself."

Emma looked at the plane, then around them at the incredible landscape, and finally, back at Rafe. Without taking her eyes off him, she said to the pilot, "The two of us can stay."

"Only one of you needs to," the pilot said.

"But two of us are going to." Rafe held Emma's gaze.

"Thank you," their pilot said sincerely, clearly relieved to have the problem solved without trouble.

Rafe smiled at Emma, who smiled back, albeit tremulously.

She was unsure and, honestly, he felt the same.

They had a large expanse of time stretching out in front of them, to do whatever they wanted.

The only problem was, he wasn't sure it would be long enough.

THE TRUCKEE/TAHOE AIRPORT was about ten miles outside of Lake Tahoe, in the small, quaint town of Truckee. They'd gotten hotel rooms, found the town, and had changed before going for dinner. They decided on the restaurant in the lovely hotel downtown where they were staying, a historical building rich in Old West detail. Their waitress told them that one hundred years ago, there'd been saloon fights in the dining room on a daily basis and a brothel upstairs.

Now, after years of neglect, the place had been recently renovated. With its buttery walls and soft lighting, it was a perfect setting for intimate dining.

But Emma didn't know if she was ready for intimate.

Before they had come in here, they'd walked around downtown. Commercial Row was filled with galleries, eateries and unique little shops that had kept them entertained for a few hours. Now darkness had fallen, cloaking them in that strange sense of isolation Rafe always provided.

She sipped her wine while they waited for their food, and looked at the tall, dark and mouthwateringly gorgeous man sitting across from her. With the candlelight glowing over his dark, dark hair and his rugged, tanned features, she could imagine him sitting there one hundred years ago, looking for trouble, then possibly going upstairs to visit the brothel.

She'd never looked for trouble a single day of her life, and yet here she was herself, courting it. Right upstairs were their rooms where they could go and finish what they started.

She could be in his arms for an entire night... Oh, yes, definitely trouble as she'd never experienced it before.

Her body hummed in anticipation, her pulse thumped a dull, heavy beat that echoed in her ears. Even her skin twitched, along with every erogenous zone in her body, of which there appeared to be more than she could have imagined.

"My sisters would love this place." Rafe looked around him at the walls that had historical prints and antique mining tools mounted on them.

This fascinated her, the thought of Rafe as a family man. "Do you see them a lot?"

"When I'm home. Which I rarely am." He smiled. "But yeah, we hang out. We like each other. Or we did." He laughed. "Now that I'll be home more, I'll be in their hair driving them crazy, making them wonder why they ever wanted me to travel less."

"How will you drive them crazy?"

His smile widened just a bit wickedly. "Oh, I'll have fun torturing Carolyn's dates. I can't do that to Tessa anymore—she's married with a baby on the way—but I'll find ways to get her, too. I'll probably buy my soon-to-arrive niece or nephew a drum set or a tuba.''

''But...those are loud instruments.''

''Yeah.'' He grinned so disarmingly that she found herself grinning back.

''I'm trying to imagine you as an obnoxious brother,'' she said.

''I'm good at it.''

''What do they do back to you?''

''Mostly just keep track of my every indiscretion. They say they're going to use it all against me someday when I have a wife and kids.''

He didn't look worried, but...happy. She tried to imagine the sort of easy love he was describing. It didn't apply to her own family. ''I used to pretend my sister and I were like that,'' she said. ''Close. Loving.''

''I thought all twins were close.''

''Oh, we're close.'' She frowned into her wine. Close as in she was always there for Amber.

But who was there for her? ''Just in a different sort of way,'' she said.

''Such as one of you needing the other one to constantly get her out of messes?''

''She's not a bad person.''

''Not at all,'' he agreed, and his fingers stroked hers. ''But if I had to guess, it's got to be more of a parental relationship, with you being the parent.''

That was it exactly. ''Yes.''

Bringing their joined hands up to his mouth, he kissed her palm, and brought her flutters right back. "What about your parents?"

"My dad died before we were born. And my mother... She's a writer, too. Literary fiction," she clarified. "The important stuff. What we do confuses her. I guess I can see that—having one daughter who tends to take off her clothes for the camera, any camera, and another daughter who wastes trees for a living—"

He gaped and tightened his fingers on her hand. "Your mother said your writing is a waste of trees?"

"Well—" she laughed, embarrassed to have let that slip "—all she meant was that what she does is very different than what I do."

"Uh-huh. I wonder if you translated your ratings into readers, how many millions you'd beat her by."

"She has a Pulitzer."

"And you're writing for television. Does she realize how hard that is?"

"All I'm saying is that sometimes we...disappoint her," she said. "Granted, Amber more often than me, but—"

"So, as a result, you spend your time running around covering Amber's ass."

"Yes, but at least she loves me for it."

"I'm sure she does. But Emma, who's there when *you* need someone?"

She stared at him, a little dismayed to have him cut

right to her inner turmoil so effortlessly. "I—I don't know." She pulled her hand free and rubbed her temple. "I don't think about it like that."

His eyes never left her as he took her hand back and lightly scraped his teeth over the fleshy part of her palm before soothing it with the tip of his tongue.

All her bones dissolved. "Rafe."

He did it again.

Her mouth went dry and she gulped down some water as her thoughts jumped ahead to what could happen next. Would he kiss her? Would he touch her—

"What are you thinking?" He stopped her nervous fingers from playing with the condensation on her glass by putting his hand over hers.

What was she thinking? She was thinking how he would feel filling her body. "Um… Well." A knowing light came into his eyes and she had to let out a little laugh that was a good part nerves. "Why ask if you already know?"

Cocking his head, he studied her with those eyes that seemed to see right through her exterior to the real Emma beneath. The one that wanted to toss the "research" facade out the window and admit she wanted him. She just wanted him, plain and simple.

And she wanted him to want her back, plain and simple. No complications, no emotional ties, nothing to bog it down, even while she knew that there was nothing plain and simple about this at all.

All around them were people dining, paying them no attention whatsoever, but she leaned in. "What's going to happen?"

"What do you want to happen?"

"Everything," she said honestly, and blinked when he choked out a laugh.

"God, Emma." He squeezed her fingers. "Do you have any idea what your honesty does to me?"

"No, but I know what all these thoughts are doing to me." She showed him the goose bumps on her arms, leaning back to do so, but noticed that his gaze landed on her breasts instead. Her nipples had responded to both his presence and her thoughts, pebbling hard against the material of her sweater as if begging for attention.

Maybe it was the wine, maybe it was the look on his face, but the room started to spin. "Oh boy. I hope our food comes soon."

"Emma." His voice was hoarse. "Tell me you aren't too toasted for this, because I plan to slowly strip you so I can taste every single inch of you, something I can't do if you're tipsy."

"Why not?" She heard the wispy hopefulness in her voice. Later she could be horrified by that, but right now, with the room spinning feverishly and her body hot and achy, she couldn't think that far.

"Because I want you one hundred percent with me."

She eyed him as she tried to put words to her thoughts. "I had no idea you were so sweet."

''Would a 'sweet' guy ask you this...'' Leaning in close, he put his mouth to her ear. ''Why have you never come with a man before?''

She pulled back and stared at him. ''I...did at the pool. With you.''

''Before that.''

''Oh. I...''

''Here you go,'' said their waitress as she came toward them with their order. ''Enjoy your meal. Anything else?''

Rafe didn't take his eyes off Emma. ''No, thank you.''

With a nod, she walked away.

Rafe squeezed Emma's fingers. ''So, tell me. Why?''

13

EMMA OPENED HER MOUTH, then closed it. She didn't have a ready answer.

"Emma?"

She picked up a french fry. "I'm thinking."

Instead of pushing as she'd expected, he leaned back and eyed his plate. "I can't remember why I wanted food. All I want to eat is you."

Her fry fell from her fingers, her entire body quivering.

He shot her a grim smile. He picked up her fry and brought it to her lips for her. When she sucked it into her mouth, he groaned.

Because she loved the sound of his torture, because her body was pulsing and having all sorts of interesting reactions, she then sucked on his finger as well.

He stared at her mouth while she did. "You're teasing me."

"Am I?"

"Yes. Is it so you don't have to answer my question?"

"Yes, could you pretend not to notice?"

"If you don't stop."

Feeling shameless, she slipped her foot out of her sandal beneath the table and rubbed his calf with her toes. The white tablecloth was thankfully long, covering her shenanigans. She lifted her leg and ran her toes up the inside of his thigh, settling them directly on the V of his jeans, smiling at his sharp intake of breath.

Beneath the ball of her foot she could feel an extremely interesting response. When she pressed lightly, he let out an inarticulate noise and wrapped his hand around her ankle. "Two can play this game." He let his other hand slip beneath the table, and since she had one leg virtually in his lap, now being held there by his firm grip on her ankle, that left her thighs wide open.

Thank goodness they were in a cozy, round corner table, close together, because when she felt his fingers slip under the material of her wide, gauzy skirt, easily bunching it up as he skimmed his palm up her inner thigh, she gasped. "Rafe—"

"That's my name," he said lightly, his knuckles barely brushing her panties in a light caress that sent her pulse racing. "So…about why you've never come with a man before…"

"I—" He still had her ankle in his grip, and while she could have asked him to stop, she didn't. She was wide open to his touch, vulnerable and unbearably aroused by it. "I like my control," she said.

"Control issues." He nodded. "We all have them.

But you, Emma—" Another light brush of his knuckles over her panties, which were quickly getting damp "—you're a tight case. You don't like people to get too close and I used to think maybe that was because you'd been hurt before, by a man. But now I think it's because you've spent your entire life trying to please someone you'll never be able to please." He spread open his hand so that his fingertips rested extremely low on her belly, which left his thumb free. He glided it right over the spot designed to make her come undone.

She nearly did.

"What I find fascinating," he said in that same conversational tone, as if they were discussing whether she wanted ketchup or mustard on her burger, "is that you've never really managed to keep that control with me."

Nothing in her life had prepared her for this situation, for this man, for these feelings. But he was right. Always, at least up until now, she'd held people at a certain distance, even while at the same time craving some sort of emotional tie. Her mother, the men she'd dated here and there, even her sister. Maybe that was why she always saved Amber—it means she was in charge. An unsettling thought.

And yet here she was at Lake Tahoe, alone with the one man who could take her hard-earned control and let it fly in the wind, sitting at a rather crowded restaurant with his hand under her skirt, his fingers stroking her halfway to orgasmic bliss.

"Emma." His index finger traced the edging of her panties, which she hoped to God weren't plain white cotton. She couldn't remember.

"Y—yes?"

"Why me?" Then that finger, the center of her universe, slipped beneath the elastic edging and once, just once, stroked over her bare flesh.

"Um—" Another stroke, and her hips arched. "*Rafe.*" Blindly she reached for purchase, gripping the table, nearly upending their drinks. "I can't think when you're doing that."

"You came with me," he said, and there was no mistaking the satisfaction in his rich voice.

"That one time—"

Another stroke of the knowing, talented finger. Then he slipped a second finger under her panties as well, using his thumb to twist the material away from her, leaving her open and exposed to his exploration. When he felt at how wet she was, he groaned.

"You think I couldn't help you come again?" he murmured.

She stared at him. He hadn't said he could *make* her come, which would imply he had all the control, but that he'd *help.*

He wanted her to know she had the control, even if it didn't feel like it at the moment.

"I could," he said softly as his fingers traced intimately over her.

She had to blink rapidly to keep him in focus and, though she'd been biting her lip, every time he slid his finger into her and then back out, a little gasping pant escaped her lips.

"You're the sexiest thing I've ever seen," he whispered, and dipped into her again.

As unbelievable as it seemed, he was right, he could help her come again, with such little effort that it should horrify her.

Instead, she was only afraid he wouldn't, that he'd somehow withhold it, leaving her like this, all trembling and aching and desperate, so she slid both her hands beneath the table, grasped his wrist and held his hand to her.

"Oh, I'm going to give you what you want," he promised her with such tenderness that she nearly burst into tears.

But with one last pass of his thumb over her swollen, wet, hot flesh, he pulled his hand free. Unable to help herself, she let out a little cry. Bold in a way she never could have imagined herself, she reached out beneath the table, gripped his thigh and ran her hand up until she could cup his rigid erection through his jeans.

He hissed in a breath and, without breaking eye contact with her, lifted his hand for the waitress and said, "Check, please."

His voice was nearly gone. Beneath her hand, he was hard and pulsing with life. Holding her gaze he brought his first finger up to his lips, the one that had been inside her, and sucked it into his mouth.

Her thighs clenched together.

"Now I know what you taste like," he murmured. "I want more, Emma."

The waitress came with their bill. Rafe tossed down some cash, then pulled her out of the restaurant into the hotel lobby.

Her body was on high alert.

"Upstairs?" he asked in a tight voice.

"God, yes."

She couldn't wait to get to one of their rooms and have him ease this ache between her legs, couldn't wait to make him as crazy as he'd made her.

They headed toward the front desk and the elevators beyond, and as they approached, the man already there turned to face them.

Their pilot.

He smiled in relief. "There you are. I felt so bad about what happened, I turned around and came right back for you. So...let's hit it."

THE PLANE RIDE wasn't as awkward as Emma might have imagined it would be. For one thing, she couldn't keep her eyes open and, fight as she might to stay awake, she kept drifting off, only to jerk awake again when her head would fall forward.

"Here." Slipping his arm around her, Rafe eased her head onto his shoulder. "Better?"

"Thank you," she whispered, suddenly not quite as tired as she'd been a minute ago. Beneath her ear she could feel the steady beat of his heart. He ran his fingers up and down her arm in a caressing motion that had her sighing.

"I'm sorry we were interrupted," he said, his cheek against her hair. "Are you okay?"

She would be. When she got home and into her own bed, when she could convince herself that she hadn't really allowed him to touch her so intimately, that she hadn't really been on the verge of an orgasm in a restaurant.

Her eyes were closed to the dark, dark night as they flew down the middle of California. "I'm pretty sure I'll have no problem being able to sum up the feelings I need for the script this week. I'm envisioning lots of heat and frustration and thwarted efforts, but then again, that's what the research was for, right?"

On her arms, his fingers went still. Beneath her cheek she felt his body tense.

"Good," he said, his voice just a little cool, and a little…sarcastic? "Glad to be of service, wouldn't want any of the time we spent to go to waste."

She lifted her head and looked at him. But the only light in the plane was from the cockpit, so his face was in the shadows.

"Go to sleep, Emma. It's been a long day."

She didn't have to see him to sense his distance, or the obvious fact that he didn't intend to talk. Fine. No talking worked for her just fine. Besides, it wasn't as if they were a couple. They'd made that perfectly clear.

He wanted her physically.

She wanted the same thing.

End of story.

So why sleep never came, why she lay there still and confused and a little sad, she had no idea.

TWO DAYS LATER Rafe's house was invaded by his family, who'd shown up with the makings of a barbecue and housewarming presents.

Rafe stood in his kitchen, leaning against the island and nursing a beer, watching as Carolyn tried to boss Tessa into chopping the vegetables.

But Tessa didn't want to do anything other than smile at her husband, Reilly, who was looking pretty smitten himself.

In the past, his sisters had always turned to Rafe for…well, everything, so it felt odd to not be needed anymore. Odd, but good. Now Reilly had to fix Tessa's car when it needed fixing. Reilly had to get the big, black hairy spiders when she found them. And Rafe knew it had been Reilly who'd put that extremely satisfied smile on her face.

Tessa found an excuse to brush by her husband, and tipped her face up in a silent demand for a kiss. When her husband instantly responded, Carolyn turned to Rafe with a roll of her eyes.

"They've been married for months and they still can't keep their hands off each other."

Rafe happened to know firsthand that you didn't have to be married to someone to be unable to keep your hands to yourself. And though he'd tried not to, he thought of Emma.

He hadn't been able to keep his hands off her.

She'd hurt him a few nights ago, though he was quite certain she didn't understand why. Hell, *he* hardly understood. But one thing he did know—the more time he spent with her, the more he wanted.

Emotional attachments scared her, and what they had together definitely fit the definition of *emotional attachment.*

Or it could.

If she'd let it.

A fact that should have scared him but didn't.

"So when are you going to tell me what's the matter?" Carolyn joined him against the island with her own drink and eyed the two oblivious lovebirds. "They driving you crazy?"

"Nah. She deserves the happiness. And Reilly's a good guy."

"True." Carolyn sighed. "But it'd be nice to find that for myself." She faced him. "And for you. Is that it? Is that what's bugging you?"

What was bothering him was a bad case of DSB—

deadly sperm build-up. He took a long pull of his beer. "Maybe."

"So, get a woman. It can't be difficult, they fall all over you regularly."

"It's not that simple."

"Why not?"

"Because I want a woman who wants *me*. Not for how I make her look on film, or how I make her feel in the bedroom, but for me. I want a woman who puts our relationship before anything else."

"Don't tell me you want her barefoot and pregnant, or I'll have to smack you."

"No," he said, but laughed. "I want her to have her own hopes and dreams and life, of course. I just want to be a big part of it. I want to be important to her."

"Oh, Rafe." Her smile was sad as she cupped his cheek. "I never really pictured being surrounded by supermodels as tough—but you're lonely, aren't you?"

He laughed again. "I'm not that bad off."

She hugged him hard, anyway. "I can see why you'd want a woman not quite so…ambitious as all the women you deal with."

"And I want her to want me whether I'm still taking pictures or working bagging groceries. You know, for better or worse."

Carolyn lay her head on his shoulder. "Have you met her yet?"

Rafe thought of Emma. He knew she didn't want him for how he made her look on film, but she did want him for how he made her feel physically.

Could there be more?

He thought of her workaholic lifestyle, how she seemed to want to be with him only when he was bringing her pleasure, and his stomach twisted a little.

''No,'' he said a little unevenly. ''I haven't met her yet.''

RAFE WENT INTO THE STUDIO they'd rented for the next two shoots, both of which were indoors. First up, a schoolgirl shot, followed by a nurse shot—two of the most popular men's fantasies, according to recent polls. And for the first time since Rafe had started this calendar, he hoped it was Amber who showed up.

Amber, he could ignore.

With Amber, he could avoid being sidetracked by any unwanted attraction.

Amber, whom he could send home afterward and forget about.

''We're ready.'' Stone had set up the lighting and cameras. ''I figure if we do it right, we can get both these shoots today. What do you think?''

What did he think? That he wished he was at home being bitched at by Puddles for more food, that he was working in his darkroom...anything. Hell, even pulling the weeds in the front yard would be better than this.

Stone took one last look at their set, a mock-up of a school hallway, complete with lockers, and nodded. "I'll go get her."

"You've seen her already, then?"

Stone stopped and eyed his longtime friend. "Yes, as a matter of fact, I have. She's in makeup with Jen."

"And..."

Stone looked amused. "And what?"

"Damn it, which one is she?"

Stone looked him over for another moment. "Which one were you hoping for?"

Rafe stared at him, then let out a breath. "I haven't a frigging clue."

Now Stone grinned. "Sure you do. Amber is gorgeous, feisty, hot and a pain in the ass. She's also possibly certifiable. But Emma..." He arched his brows. "Brains and looks. And while not a pain in the ass or certifiable, she scares you to death. So my guess would be, given the look in your eyes, you're hoping for Amber." He crossed his arms and cocked his head. "How am I doing?"

Rafe turned away. "Just go get her."

Stone laughed. "Pretty good, I'm guessing."

Two minutes later he was back, with their model for the day. Rafe was turned away from them, messing with the camera that was already perfectly set up, and not until Stone called out "Ready" did he turn and look.

Her long hair had been divided into two braids. She

wore a white button-down shirt, crisply ironed and completely unbuttoned, revealing a white crop top beneath. Her black-and-white plaid skirt was wraparound and so short he couldn't imagine it fully covered her butt in the back, but since he couldn't see, he couldn't be sure. She wore white knee socks, one pushed down, the other up to her knee, and black clunky boots. The epitome of the naughty schoolgirl.

He'd avoided looking into her face, but he looked now, and his heart took one quick heavy kick.

Emma.

Stone's pager went off. He looked down at the pager, took in the message and swore.

Rafe jerked his head toward Stone, and at the look on his friend's face, his stomach dropped. "No."

"Sorry, buddy." Stone grimaced. "Crystal's in labor. Gotta run."

Rafe knew Stone's sister hadn't planned the worst possible moment to go into labor on purpose, but the timing couldn't have been more off. "But—"

"I'll call you," Stone said, and he left.

The door to the studio closing seemed extraordinarily loud.

"Where do you want me?" Emma asked softly when the awkward silence had gone on for nearly a full minute.

"Where do I want you?" He looked at her from beneath heavy lidded eyes, wondering how the hell he was supposed to answer that question without sending her running.

"For the shot," she clarified.

"Ah. For the shot."

"You do need it, right?"

"Sure. But why isn't Amber here, Emma?"

"She's…busy."

"Really? Because I know she's back in the country. She called Stone. She could have come, but she didn't. I find that fascinating."

"I…" She let out a pent-up breath, and that, of course, drew his eyes to her breasts, which were nearly popping out of the crop top.

His body twitched. Damn it.

"I thought I should come," she whispered, and tugged at the short, short skirt.

"More research today? For your work?"

"I wanted…to thank you for dinner that night in Tahoe."

"Thank me." He laughed. "You wanted to thank me for feeling you up at the table?"

She crossed her arms, which only plumped up those mouthwatering breasts all the more. "You're still mad at me."

"Mad?" He shook his head. "No."

"Then, why are you pouting?"

"*Pouting?*"

"Sulking, then."

"I'm doing no such thing."

"Look, maybe we should just do this."

He knew what he wanted to do. *Her.* "Fine. Get up against the lockers, lean in close like you're going to kiss 'em, stick your ass out and look back at me over your shoulder."

"All business?" she asked softly.

It was that or grab her. "All business."

But he hadn't counted on having to put his camera down and walk up to her, leaning so enticingly on the lockers, so he could drape her hair over her bare shoulder—bare because the white shirt had slipped off one side. She gleamed and sparkled from whatever lotion they'd put on her. He'd been wrong about the skirt—it just covered her ass and was slightly crooked. He put his hands on her hips and adjusted it, ignoring her quickened breathing. That didn't work so he had to tug on the hem, which had his fingers brushing the very bottom of her sweet cheeks.

She let out a sound that had him jerking his gaze to hers, but she didn't look at him. She just stared at the lockers, her chest rising and falling rapidly, as if she could barely stand it.

Join the club, baby, he thought grimly. Without a word, he went back to his camera and starting shooting, talking to her only when necessary. She never loosened up, not as he'd been able to coax her to do on the other shoots, but today he just didn't have it in him.

Some professional.

"Turn toward me," he instructed. "Hands flat on the lockers at your side. Tilt your head down, eyes up at me."

Without a word, she did, and he took those shots, too. Her slight stiffness actually worked in his favor—she was the slightly shy, slightly reticent, outrageously sexy schoolgirl. It was wrong, but he wanted her, wanted so damn much. By the time he put the camera down, his fingers were shaking.

"Is that it?" she asked, still against the lockers.

"That's it."

She pushed away and walked toward him, every sway of her hips a slam to his gut.

"What are you doing?" he asked, and backed up a step.

She didn't stop until their toes touched. "I didn't like that."

"I didn't, either."

She cocked a hip and looked at him from carefully made-up eyes. "I don't like you, either."

"Ditto," he said tightly.

"But I've never wanted you more," she said in a frustrated voice.

Thank God. They lunged at each other.

14

THEY COULDN'T GET AT EACH OTHER fast enough. Rafe slammed his mouth down on Emma's, open and hot and hungry. Given the sexy little growl that came from her throat, she felt the same way he did. She wrapped her arms around his neck, her legs around his waist, just as he cupped a sweet, warm, rounded cheek in each hand and ground her against him.

Baby, oh baby, it was just what the doctor had ordered.

His head was still spinning. Just a moment before, he'd been furious with her, furious and desperate with the excitement she always stirred within him just beneath the surface, and now here she was, arching against him, opening her legs up even wider, which had her short skirt hiked up around her waist, leaving nothing but his jeans and her thin panties as barriers. When she rocked against him, he staggered, and might have dropped them both to the floor if he hadn't backed to the wall to use it as support.

Her fingers tangled in his hair and held his head for her mouth. Her legs were stronger than he could have imagined, gripping around him so that he couldn't leave.

As if he wanted to.

When she arched into him again releasing a helpless whimper into his mouth, he nearly whimpered back because he couldn't touch her, holding her up as he was; he couldn't get to her the way he wanted to. Instead he staggered away from the wall and carried her into the open prop room. Kicking the door closed with his foot, he reversed their positions, turning them so that she was the one with her back to the wall. Now he could thrust against her in mindless abandon. With her skirt bunched up around her waist and his fingers inside the back of her panties, the apex of her legs cradling his sex like a hot glove, he could hardly stand it.

Bracing her against the wall, he tugged the white button-down shirt off her shoulders, then slid the twin thin straps of her crop down as well. Since she didn't have on a bra, her breasts spilled free, her nipples already tight and puckered. Even that wasn't enough, so he reached down and dragged her panties aside. Wrenching his mouth free from hers, he looked at her glorious body. The erotic way he'd exposed her made him groan.

"You are so beautiful."

She was writhing against him, making those sexy

little noises in her throat, her lush breasts against his chest, gripping him for all she was worth.

"*Rafe.* God, Rafe, how do you do this to me every time?"

Just the way she said his name made him want to come, but he managed a low laugh. "What I'm doing to you…? Baby, it's the other way around. You're killing me, just killing me."

Now she was nibbling at his throat, taking hot bites out of him, each one making his hard-on twitch. He was pressed between her legs as they moved their hips, rubbing, rubbing, rubbing in slow circles that were going to drive him right out of his mind.

"More," she panted, and pulled his T-shirt up so that her breasts brushed against his bare chest.

His knees went a little wobbly—more so when she tried to work open the buttons on his Levi's.

"You want to come again, Emma? With me?"

"Yes!" Her fingers fumbled ineffectively on his jeans.

Reaching in, he helped her, their fingers tangling together until the jeans were open, a huge relief as they'd been cutting off his circulation since the moment she'd walked into the studio. His penis jutted out from his shorts hopefully while she continued to move those hips, driving them both closer to the brink.

"Rafe—" She pushed at his jeans, tugged at his shorts. "In me," she gasped. "Inside me now."

He wrapped a fist around himself and poised at her slick entrance before he remembered and went still.

"Rafe?"

"No condom," he said roughly.

Her eyes opened and she looked at him in trembly dismay. "*No.*"

He could only shake his head.

"I'm going to cry," she whispered.

Slowly he released her legs. Then, holding her gaze, he dropped to his knees. He put his hands beneath her skirt and pushed it up. Kissed one thigh, then the other.

Then between.

Her head thunked back against the door. "Rafe—"

He kissed her again.

Then he used his tongue.

Her knees buckled, but he held her up, and when she shattered, he let her fall into his arms.

IT TOOK HER A MOMENT to regain control of her senses, but when she did, she felt the tension that remained in his big, rigidly controlled body. "I want to nibble, too." She dropped a kiss on his right pec, over his T-shirt. With one hand on his arm, restraining him, she used her other to shove up his shirt. He was all sinewy and hard flesh, and when she put her lips just above his nipple, his muscles quivered. He let out a sound—a rough one that thrilled her—and lifted his hands toward her.

Catching them, she set them at his side and looked up at him. "No touching." She added a smile. "You've watched me go wild for you. I want to watch you go wild for me for a change."

"Shouldn't we—" He broke off with a strangled groan when she licked his nipple—just one little lick, as if he were a delectable treat. "Emma—"

"Shh." Dragging hot, wet kisses down his torso to his low belly, she paused to look up at him.

His face was a tight grimace. "Emma, we should—"

She pulled apart his unfastened jeans and kissed the spot, the tender, beautiful spot of skin she'd exposed. It wasn't tan like the rest of him, and somehow that seemed achingly vulnerable.

"Em—"

She tugged at the opening again, a little harder this time, and hummed her pleasure as his erection sprang out, hampered only by his knit boxers.

"Stone might come back—" he started to say, but he broke off with another heartfelt groan when she pulled the fabric away from his body and let him free.

He was smooth and long and thick, and she let out a murmur of excitement. "You weren't worried about that a minute ago." She ran a finger down his rigid length. Feeling incredibly empowered and bold, she kissed the very tip of him.

"Emma." His voice was no more than a harsh

whisper, so she did it again. His head fell back, his fingers tightened in her hair. "What are you doing to me?"

In truth, she wasn't quite sure. She wasn't a virgin—she'd slept with three different boyfriends, but none of them had been relationships where she'd been sexually comfortable.

And not one of them, as she'd already admitted to Rafe, had been able to bring her to orgasm.

But Rafe had and it wasn't just gratitude that had her wanting to please him orally, but a burning desire to try this, to bring him to pleasure, too, and make it her own.

His hands were fisted at his side now, his belly and legs rigid as he lay there letting her explore. She eyed the very tip of him, straining so desperately toward her mouth. It seemed no effort at all to take him inside, to run her tongue over him.

"Emma—" As if he couldn't help himself, his hands tangled in her hair. "Don't stop."

"I won't." And she didn't, not until Rafe lost the reins on his control and shuddered as helplessly as she had only moments before.

He still hadn't returned to normal breathing when suddenly, from outside the prop room door, came voices, startling them into silence.

"You say they were just here?"

Emma blinked. That was Amber's voice! What was her sister doing here?

"I said so, didn't I?" Stone sighed. "Look, I left them right in this very studio when my sister paged me thinking she was in labor. False alarm."

"Hmm...wonder how the shoot went?"

"With those two? Fireworks guaranteed."

Inside the prop closet, Emma closed her eyes. Fireworks had definitely gone off.

"What do you mean?" Amber asked.

"Don't you know?"

"Know what?" Amber's voice went from wary to annoyed. "Don't tell me he's playing with her."

"You really don't know," Stone marveled. "Well, you're going to love this. As much as you and I can't stand each other, they have the opposite problem—only, as far as I know, neither has admitted it."

Inside the prop room Rafe stared at Emma. Emma stared right back.

"They're hot for each other?" Amber went quiet for a moment. "This I can't imagine."

"Why not?"

"Because Rafe isn't hot for anyone 'Hollywood' and, although Emma isn't typical Hollywood, she works there, and her work is her life. And even if he'd lost his mind and decided to go for it, there's the little fact that Emma wouldn't want him in return. She doesn't have time for *me,* much less anyone else. She doesn't have time for anything but her writing."

"So explain why she's been acting as you on and off for the past month," Stone said.

Amber laughed. "That's simple. I begged her. I needed her help."

"You needed her help," Stone said doubtfully.

"Mmm-hmm. And just so you know, I don't...*not* like you."

Stone laughed. "That's why you tell everyone I'm gay."

"No, I tell everyone you're gay to explain the fact you don't want me."

There was silence. Then Stone said in an odd voice, "Whoever said I didn't want you?"

"You did, that night—"

"That night you came on to me when you already had a date with you? Did you ever think maybe I just didn't want to share?"

"So...what are you saying?"

"Do you have a date now?"

"You don't see one, do you?"

"Ask me now, then," he said.

A pause. "Okay. Stone, do you want me?"

"I'd like to explore the options."

There was no sound, then Stone let out a choked noise. "Why are you leaning against the lockers like that?"

"Just giving you time to explore your options." Her voice became sultry. "You know what I just realized, Stone? I think you're going to like the options."

"You still have a boyfriend?"

"I left Kenny in the Caribbean."

"I thought it was Ricardo."

"Stone, Stone. Keep up."

Stone let out a laugh that didn't sound too convincing. "Stop doing that."

"Stop doing what?"

"Stop lifting your skirt like that and showing off your thong."

"I don't think you want me to stop."

"Amber—"

"Stone," Amber mocked, then laughed. "Oh, come on. Stop resisting. Let's get the hell out of here, stud."

Stone must have agreed, because the studio door shut and suddenly the place was quiet. Embarrassed now that the afterglow had dimmed, Emma began to straighten her clothing.

She heard Rafe doing the same, though she didn't look at him.

"A damn closet," he muttered. "First a pool, then a restaurant and now a damn closet. You'd think I could manage to get you into a bed."

"They're going to see our cars in the lot," she said, crossing her arms, wishing she could say she'd never wanted to come today, wishing she could say she wished they had never started this whole thing.

But she didn't wish that at all.

"Probably," Rafe agreed.

"Maybe I should go."

He just looked at her.

"And, anyway…I have some writing to do."

"Well then, you'd better run, hadn't you." He waited until her hand was on the door. "But don't fool yourself, Emma, or even try to fool me. You running now has nothing to do with getting caught or even your precious work. I've gotten too close again and you need out. Plain and simple."

She didn't question that. Silly to, when he spoke the truth. She reached for the door.

"Emma?"

She hesitated but this time didn't look back.

"We still have to do the nurse shoot."

Damn it. "Right."

They finished the shoot in perfect silence and, when it was over and she'd changed and again reached for the door, he said softly, "See you next time."

NEXT TIME. Emma drove, the words racing through her head. What did he mean *next time?* There wasn't going to be a next time!

What had happened?

Had she really just had oral sex in a closet?

She put her shaking fingers to her mouth as she waited at a red light to get onto the freeway. She'd meant to go home, to shower and crawl into bed with her laptop, where she'd get the most out of the experience and use it to her advantage.

Instead she passed her exit and drove to her sister's condo. Her sister's car wasn't there. Of course not—she was off with Stone. It wouldn't take long because Amber rarely lingered, so Emma sat on her porch and waited.

True to form, fifteen minutes later Amber pulled up in her red convertible Mustang, music blaring, hair snapping in the wind, cheeks rosy from the drive.

Or possibly from her little rendezvous with Stone.

She hopped out of the car, singing to herself, grinning like the cat who'd just eaten the canary, until she saw Emma sitting there. Then her step faltered, her smile froze and a wary look came into those eyes so like Emma's own.

For one brief moment.

Then it was gone and Amber was sauntering close, swinging her hips, chewing her gum, looking like she'd just won the lotto. "Sis!"

"What happened to Kenny?"

"Well…"

"And how long have you been back in town?"

"I just…"

"And why the hell am I still doing this photo shoot

for you?'' Emma demanded, just before she horrified both of them by bursting into tears.

Amber's bravado was gone in a flash and she sat next to Emma, her voice hitching. ''Don't you start now. Don't you start. I'm not wearing waterproof mascara today.''

Emma ruthlessly swiped at the tears she hated shedding. ''I wouldn't be starting...if it weren't for you.''

''Please don't cry,'' Amber begged, looking traumatized. ''You never cry.''

''Never say never.'' Emma would have said she'd never want a man to do half of what Rafe had done to her, and she sure as hell would have said she didn't need it, or him, but it was exactly that which was keeping her up at night wondering, aching, needing.

Amber looked her over, satisfied Emma wasn't going to continue with the meltdown. ''And as for why you're doing this photo shoot for me...because you said you would! You said not to come back! You said you had it all handled! Well, honey, if I'd known that having it all handled meant you were handling Rafe, I'd have slapped some sense into you. He's not a man you want to tangle your emotions with.''

''I'm not sleeping with him.''

''Good. Because he's—''

''I know what he is, Amber,'' Emma said woodenly. ''I'm just not sure you do.''

"You're mad at me," Amber said with a sigh. "And I guess I deserve it."

"Yes," Emma agreed, then sighed. "But I do like to run our lives, don't I."

"Yes. So really, this isn't all my fault at all."

"Things are going to change, Amber. I'm sorry, but you're going to have to take over and run your own life. No more calling me to bail you out of everything—I just can't do it anymore."

Amber looked unnerved.

"Yeah, I guess I deserve that. I'll, uh, get the next fantasy shoot info."

Emma blinked. "Oh. Well—"

"There's not much left, anyway. Just September through December."

"I didn't mean you have to finish the shoot."

"What *did* you mean?"

She had no idea.

"Don't worry about it," Amber said. "I think it's the Harley-Davidson bike shoot next. Probably if I'd checked my calendar or with my agent, I'd know that already. But we both know how good I am at organization." She let out a gusty sigh. "I guess I'm going to have to get better at that, too."

Surprising them both, she leaned over and hugged Emma, who could count on one hand the times Amber had ever done so.

"Don't be mad at me anymore."

Emma hugged her back. "I'm not mad at you, I'm mad at me."

"Because you've been boning Rafe?"

"I haven't been—" She broke off rather than confess. "We should be talking about you. You were with Stone today."

Amber laughed. "We needed to get it out of our systems. And boy, did we have fun doing that. We're done now."

If only it were that easy for Emma.

"So, about that motorcycle shoot—"

"I'll take care of it," Emma said, a little too quickly.

"But you just said—"

"I know. Don't listen to me."

Amber stared at her, then pulled back to get a better look. "What's up? Is Stone right about the two of you being crazy about each other?"

Well, they were *something* for each other. And quite frankly, *crazy* just might be the right word.

But in any case, she wasn't ready to put it into words. "Amber, you know how you got along in life just...winging it?"

Amber laughed. "Yes. It's a particular specialty of mine."

"And you know how you're always saying I should try the same?"

"You're not telling me you're going to start winging it, not with this man. Oh, no, because honey, you're supposed to start with something small at first. Say, like…going to the grocery store without an alphabetized list. *Then* you can slowly work your way up to the top, to an advanced run. Rafe, now *he's* an advanced run. Double diamond, baby. Do you know what I'm saying?"

Emma knew what she was saying.

But it was too late.

"I have a thing for motorcycles," she said to Amber. "A secret…fantasy thing."

"Really?"

"Really." Okay, maybe not really.

But she had her eye on the advanced run—the double diamond—and nothing else would do.

15

RAFE WALKED THROUGH HIS HOUSE, his pretty neighbor Irena at his side, taking notes on what he wanted to do to each room.

"I'm so glad we're finally getting together to do this," she said, and shot him a little smile.

It had taken him a few weeks to get in touch with her. He'd planned on doing everything for the house himself but found he was tired of living in such a sterile-looking place. "I still have a month or so of work left, but I thought we could at least get the ball rolling."

"I'd hoped you would call. I've been looking so forward to working with you." She was dressed in blue trousers with a crisp white blouse that made him think of June Cleaver.

Wife material, a small voice inside his head said. *And she's looking at you as if she wants to gobble you up.*

Let her.

Instead, he kept his distance, not wanting to give off the wrong signal before he was ready.

And he wouldn't be ready until he got Emma out of his head, if that was even possible.

"You're going to love having the place fixed up," she said, sidling closer. "We'll make it a home."

He was counting on that. Only four more shoots for the fantasy calendar and he'd be done.

Free.

He would be able to hang around and enjoy himself. Do whatever struck his fancy.

Irena's face was tipped down now as she concentrated on the notes she was making on her pad, exposing her neck and throat. He tried, he really did, to feel attracted to her. To want to kiss her. After all, she lived right across the street. She was kind and sweet, she had her own life and, most of all, she was clearly attracted to him.

Maybe if he could get a certain Emma Willis out of his head, he could handle this better. Emma, the little workaholic, the woman who ran scared every time he tried to get closer than sex.

There, that helped a little, remembering that.

They moved into the master bedroom now, which held his bed and a dresser and not much else. "I figure this room needs something," he said. "But I can't quite figure out what—"

A brown-and-gray ball of fur leaped to the bed and stared at him defiantly, as if daring him to make her get down.

"Hey, flea-ball, that's my bed," he said, knowing

damn well she didn't have fleas because just last night he'd finally been able to bathe her. The experience had left them both soaking wet and grumpy, but it had been worth it. Now she didn't smell like three-week-old garbage.

She only looked like it.

Irena tossed her notes to the mattress and sat next to the cat, stroking her until the lazy little thing sprawled out over his covers and eyed him as if to say, *You fool, you could have her stroking you, too, if you played your cards right.*

"I have some great ideas for this room," Irena said, and patted the bed next to her. "Sit. I'll show you."

"Well, I—"

"Sit, silly." And she pulled him down next to her.

From the front of the house, his doorbell rang. Rafe assumed it was Stone with the proofs he'd been waiting on. Since he'd left the door open on purpose, Rafe called out, "Back here!"

"Look at this." Irena set the pad in his lap and leaned in close, pointing to the paper, making sure her hair fell away, exposing her cleavage. "I thought we could—"

"Oh." Not Stone, but Emma stood in the doorway to his bedroom, wearing jean shorts and a white T-shirt, hair down, no makeup, and looking so far from the hot, sexy model he'd gotten used to that for a second he just blinked at her.

She was staring at him sitting on the bed next to

Irena with a carefully blank expression on her face. ‘‘Excuse me, I thought you said to come in.’’

‘‘I did. I—’’ Rafe didn’t understand the flash of guilt that went through him, because, damn it, he had done nothing wrong. But he didn’t have time to wallow in it because Emma was already gone. ‘‘Emma!’’

‘‘Who’s that?’’ asked Irena, halting him at the bedroom door with her soft voice.

He looked back at her sitting on his bed, just as his front door slammed. *Ouch.* He had no idea what Emma had wanted or needed, but one thing was certain. Whatever she’d come for, he’d never get it out of her now.

‘‘Can you excuse me a minute?’’

He reached the porch steps just as Emma’s car door slammed shut as well. He planted himself in front of her car as she put it into gear, hoping she wasn’t mad enough to run him over.

Through her windshield, she waved him aside.

Because of the sun’s glare he couldn’t see her expression, but that was probably a good thing. He held his ground and shook his head.

She rolled down her window. ‘‘Move,’’ she said, and revved her engine.

At least she’d put it in neutral to do so. Since he knew if he moved aside to walk up to the driver’s window she’d either drive away or run over his feet, he instead came right at her, stopping when his thighs brushed the front of her car. With his hands on the hood, he leaned in until he got past the sun's glare and could see her expression good and clear.

He'd expected anger. He'd expected aloofness, neither of which he felt he deserved, but that's what he figured he'd get.

He did not count on misery. "Come on out, let's talk."

"You're busy."

"I'm never too busy for you," he said, shocked to find that utterly true.

She blinked once, slowly. "Your girlfriend might disagree."

"Actually, I'm the neighbor, not the girlfriend." Irena came into the street, ran a hand over Rafe's back and smiled at him. "But I can certainly see you're a little preoccupied. We'll finish the design stuff later, whenever you're ready." And then she started walking across the street. She eyed Emma with curiosity but didn't say another word and, a moment later, vanished inside her house.

Rafe hadn't removed his gaze from Emma, so he saw her roll her eyes at herself, mutter something, and then, reluctantly, with a good amount of humility in her gaze, look at him.

"She's your neighbor. She's a designer."

"That's right." Suddenly enjoying himself, he leaned on the hood of her car as if he had all the time in the world. "Who did you think she was?"

"You were on your bed," Emma said.

''We were going through the entire house, taking notes. But you know what's fascinating, Emma? That you cared I had a woman in my room. It's quite revealing, actually.''

She rolled her eyes again, but didn't rev the engine.

''You know what I think?'' he asked.

''No, and I don't want to know.''

''I think you were jealous.''

''I was not. I don't have a jealous bone in my body.''

He decided to let that one go, because he had an even more interesting question. ''Why are you here?''

''Because...I needed to know about the next photo shoot.''

''But Amber's back in town.''

''Yeah.''

''So it would have nothing to do with you.''

''Right.'' She closed her eyes. ''I keep forgetting that part.''

''In any case, why didn't you just call Stone for the info?''

''Because... Oh, just never mind.'' Looking flustered, adorable and pathetic all in one bundle, she rested her head on the steering wheel.

And that's when he made his move. He came around to the side of her car. He reached in and turned off the engine, removing her keys. Then he shoved them into his pocket. Opening her door, he hunkered at her side.

She still had her head down. ''Go away.''

''You came to see me.'' He was still marveling over that. Because he couldn't keep his hands off her for another second, he stroked her hair. ''Do you have any idea how much that means to me?''

Craning her neck, she eyed him from under her arm. ''So I came to see you. So what. It was stupid.''

''No, it wasn't. But I'd like to hear the real reason why. Without hiding behind work, without hiding behind any excuse at all.''

''But I don't know why.''

''Come on.''

She drew in a deep breath. ''Fine. I just wanted to see you.''

''There.'' He unhooked her seat belt. ''Was that so difficult?''

''Actually, yes.''

Laughing, he stood and pulled her out of the car. ''Poor baby. Well, let's make it even, then. I'm glad you came. I don't know why, but there it is.''

She stared at him as if he was crazy. ''You're the strangest man I've ever met.''

''But you want me.''

They stood facing each other in the middle of the street, Rafe holding on to her wrist just in case she decided to try bolting again.

''Yes,'' she admitted, not sounding very happy about it. ''I want you. We're too different and we would probably kill each other in the long term, but I'm not talking long term when I say I want you."

"What are you talking?"

"Short term. Very short term."

He nodded. "As far as honesty goes, you're pretty good at it."

"So what now, Rafe?"

"Have you ever wanted a man before?"

"Of course I have."

"No, I mean *really* wanted."

She stared at him, pride warring with honesty, but honesty won. "No. Not like this."

He softened both his hold on her and his voice. "Have you ever made the first move?"

Now she looked away. "No. But I didn't think it would be this hard."

"It's not."

"Maybe *you* could do it," she suggested. "Just...I don't know... Grab me, kiss me senseless, something. Just get us started."

In all his life, he'd never felt so absolutely tender toward a woman. He wanted to do everything she'd said, but he shook his head regretfully. "I think you should do this. I think you need to do this."

"Fine. Here goes." She closed her eyes for a moment, then opened them. "Do you want to go inside? Maybe get a drink and sit outside and talk or something? And not about the calendar or my work, but something else?"

''Like...what?''

She blinked. ''Like what? What do you mean 'like what'? I just want to go inside.''

''And do what, Emma?''

''You're not making this easy.''

''And do what, Emma?'' he repeated gently.

She let out a long sigh and fixed her gaze at a spot somewhere over his shoulder. ''And finish what we've started too many times.''

''Do you mean—''

''Yes.'' She put her hands on her hips. ''So, do you want to or not?''

''So romantic,'' he said dryly, then laughed when she bared her teeth. He slipped both his hands in hers, then slowly drew them behind her back, snagging her body up to his. Holding her gaze, he leaned in, so that her breasts pressed up against his chest. Nice.

So was the way her breath caught.

''Rafe?''

''I'm sorry, what was the question again?''

''Are we going to...?''

''Yeah, that's the one.'' Though it killed him, he gave her a light kiss on the lips and lifted his head just a little. ''So you want to go inside, make love for...how did you put it? The short term.''

''Y-yes.''

''You're sure?''

''Yes.''

"Does this include you spending the night? Breakfast? What?"

Her mouth opened, then closed. She tried glaring at him, but he didn't back down.

"What are you doing?" she asked in disbelief. "Any other guy would have had me in his bed by now, naked, and you're out here clarifying the terms?"

"Yep."

"But...why?"

"Emma, when we first met, you didn't even think you could have an orgasm with a man. We proved that theory wrong. Now, the way I see it, the only hurdle left is proving you can trust one." He slid his jaw along hers. "Trust me," he whispered. "Start this, instead of being led into it. Start it—show me what you want, without any of the fantasies from the photo shoot. It's just you and me now. Just tell me what you want. Tell me and then trust me to give it to you."

"All right," she said.

She snaked her arms around his neck and put her mouth to his ear. She let out a slow breath, as if garnering her courage, and it had him hard in two seconds flat.

Then she pulled back, looked him right in the eyes and said, "I want you. I want you naked. I want you naked inside of me. I want to come with you like that. As for after that...I'd like to try something new—I'd like to wing it."

She gave a smile that was just a tad unsure, and also the most arousing, sensual thing he'd ever seen.

"How am I doing?" she whispered when he'd just stared at her for several moments.

"Good," he said, and still didn't move. "Really good."

Finally, she let out a laugh. "So? Can we? Now? Right now?"

"Yes," he said. "Right now."

16

TOGETHER THEY TURNED toward Rafe's house, just as a motorcycle came down the street. Emma could barely breathe with all the thoughts of what Rafe was about to do to her whirling in her head. But then he stopped, swore roughly, and took her hand and tugged her back toward her car.

"What's the matter?" He'd changed his mind. He didn't want her. He was going to send her home, where she'd spend yet another night tossing and turning, unfulfilled, aching...

"See that bike over there? That's Stone." He opened the passenger door. "Do you want to drive or should I?"

"Where?"

"Anywhere, quick. Unless you want to stay here and forget about—"

"No," she said. She wasn't forgetting about anything, thank you very much. She'd come for some sort of end to this terrible yearning and anticipation and she wasn't letting him out of her sight until she got it. "You can drive."

She watched as he came around and got in swearing

when his knees bumped the steering wheel. Sliding the seat back, he started the car and drove off.

On the bike, Stone craned his neck to watch them go, waving when they passed.

Rafe didn't wave back. Jaw tight, working the temperamental gear shift as if he'd been driving this vehicle all his life, he sped away.

Emma stared at his hand on the gear stick. It was big, tanned and, she had good reason to know, calloused on his fingertips and palm. Just thinking about how that warm hand felt gliding over her breast, catching a little on her nipple, made her shiver.

"Which way?" he asked.

Feeling suddenly dry-mouthed, she just pointed.

While his long legs worked the clutch and the gas, his face was taut with concentration…and something else, something making his big, hard body tight with tension.

He glanced over at her with so much hunger and heat in his eyes, it took her breath.

Excitement flooded through her, making her nipples even harder, and between her legs she was already wet. He hadn't even touched her yet, but oh, he was going to, and all because she'd asked him. She'd come on to him and he'd not only accepted, he couldn't wait to get to it.

The power of that was mind-blowing. "Here," she said, pointing. "You turn here."

He did so fast and furiously, as if on a car chase.

She couldn't help it—a little laugh escaped her, though she wasn't sure if it was from amusement or nerves.

"What?" he asked in a low voice, glancing over at her. "What's so funny?"

"Your hurry."

He spared her another glance. "You didn't think I'm dying here? That I've been dying for a very long time?"

"I'm sorry."

"Don't be. You can spend the next few hours making it all up to me."

How was it he made her want to laugh and melt at the same time? "So just to put it all out there…we're tied in the wanting department. Right?" This was her last doubt, right here. Because she knew how much she wanted him, more than her next breath, actually, and she didn't see how he could want her that much in return.

Without taking his eyes off the road, he reached over and took her hand. He brought it up to his mouth, took a quick bite out of her palm, then kissed the spot.

She felt the tug all the way to her belly.

"We are tied," he said softly, then slid her hand down his body to the juncture of his jeans, cupping his hand over hers so that she could feel the unmistakable outline of an erection so impressive it took her breath.

She stared at him, her fingers molding to the shape of him through the denim.

"I'm not going to be able to take much of that," he said, eyes still on the road.

She did it again.

"Feeling playful?" He squeezed her bare thigh before running the tips of his fingers beneath the hem of her denim shorts.

"T-turn right," she said on a shaky laugh. "Second house on the left. It's the last house on the street—"

He parked in her driveway so fast that her head spun.

"Inside," he said. As if to make sure she was following, he pulled her out across his seat.

At her front door, he waited with barely masked impatience while she fumbled with the lock. Fumbled, because there was something unsettling about having a six-foot-two-inch, gorgeously rumpled, frustrated man standing over her, breathing down her neck, needing her so badly he couldn't even talk.

She barely got the door unlocked before he took her arm and led her inside, pressing her back against the door as he shut it with their momentum. And then she was pinned there by his harder body.

"Now," he said.

"Now," she agreed.

He pulled off her shirt in one economical movement, then lifted his arms for her when she tugged at his. Both hit the floor. He went to work on her bra next, swearing when he couldn't find the hook. Laughing a little, gasping for breath, too, she showed him the hidden latch. Then it was gone and he bent, taking a breast in his mouth.

"Wait," she said.

And with his mouth on her breast and his fingers on the fastener of her shorts, he went still.

"I just thought a bed..."

With a groan, he rested his forehead against hers. "Yeah, a bed, face to face, with my body buried so deeply inside yours that I don't know where I end and you start."

Just his words made her quiver.

"But if we go now, it'll be over far too fast." He dropped to his knees and slid off her shoes and shorts, leaving her in nothing but a pair of sunshine-yellow cotton bikini panties. He ran his finger over the elastic at her hip, slid both hands around the back of her and cupped her cheeks in his hand.

"You have the best ass ever. Turn around, Emma."

Her stomach fluttered but she did as he asked—turned so that her front was now pressed up against the door. Still on his knees, he traced his fingers along the leg openings of her panties, until they met at the back juncture of her legs, lingering to explore. She pressed her palms flat to the door, and her cheek, too, looking for balance in a tilted world. Her nipples pressed against the wood, as well, and her thigh muscles were so tight they were shaking.

"Rafe—" She broke off when he touched the inside of her thigh, urging her legs open for more discovery on his part, and she had to lock her knees to remain upright.

"Mmm." One finger slid beneath the material and lightly, so lightly, traced over her every curve. "So wet."

And then he slid her panties down. She gasped and, then when she felt his mouth low on one cheek, the gasp turned into a moan. He kissed a line down to the back of one thigh and then up the other, while his fingers delved between, leaving her panting, arching, writhing.

"Please," she heard herself whisper. "Oh, please."

"Anything." Surging to his feet, he pressed his chest to her back, slipping his arms around her ribs so that he could cup her breasts, teasing her nipples into two tight, aching peaks with a rasping glide of his fingers and thumbs. "Anything, Emma."

"Inside me," she managed to say, pushing her butt into his crotch, knowing she was making the front of his jeans wet but beyond caring.

She heard the *pop, pop, pop* of his buttons. Felt him rub the length of his erection down her backside. Arching her back, thrusting herself upward to help, pressing her face to the wood, she whispered his name again—a whisper that turned into a cry of pleasure when he eased just his very tip inside her.

Then he pulled back. Thinking he was going to

thrust again, she widened her stance and waited with baited breath. He kissed her shoulder, her neck, whispering her name, and when she realized he was asking her a question, she lifted her head.

"I still don't have a condom." He kissed the other side of her neck. "I'm sorry, I didn't think when I ran out of the house after you like I did that I'd—"

"I have one," she admitted, and turned to face him. "I write city girls for a living, remember? I…thought I should know how to use one." Embarrassed, she started to look the other way, but he tilted her chin up and kissed her long and deep.

"Let's go," he said, and kicked off the rest of his clothes.

She looked down at the clothes on the floor, feeling more than a little naked, but he took her hand and tugged her toward the hall, not giving her a chance to feel anything but him.

It worked. His kiss always would. He just had a way of putting everything he had into it, and getting her to do the same. Before him, she'd have said kissing with her tongue was…well, something she tolerated.

Now? She thrived on those kisses. At least for tonight. *Just for tonight.*

She took him into her bathroom, opened the drawer and showed him the box missing one condom. A smile pulled at the corners of his mouth.

"What did you experiment on?"

"A carrot," she admitted, blushing when he laughed good and hard.

"A carrot." Shaking his head, he pulled a condom out of the box, ripped open the packet with his teeth and then handed it to her. "Show me."

"You're bigger than a carrot," she murmured as she rolled the condom down the length of him.

"Yes, thankfully."

She led him to her bedroom. She hadn't opened the shutters because the light interfered with the screen of her laptop. She hadn't picked up her clothes, and her bed wasn't made.

One of the pitfalls of working twenty-four-seven—she never got to the "home" stuff and it was never more evident than right this minute.

"Sorry," she muttered. She kicked a pile under her bed, then tossed a towel off her sheets to the floor.

"No, it's good," he said, following her down, down, down to the mattress, covering her body with his, thrusting a leg between hers so that she was wide open to him. "Emma." He took her mouth with his until she was once again clinging to him.

Then, holding her hips in his hands, he lifted up enough to snag her gaze with his.

And that just might have been her biggest mistake yet. Because as he thrust inside her with one delicious flex of his hips, as he let out a low moan that was a twin to hers, as he gathered her close, she knew the undeniable truth.

This was about far more than tonight.

This was about her heart.

About her soul.

But quite possibly, about falling in love.

But since she couldn't go there, not now, maybe not ever, she closed her eyes and let the wave of passion take them both.

17

RAFE WOKE UP at the crack of dawn to find he had one tiny corner of the bed, no covers and no pillow.

And no woman in his arms.

Emma had the rest of the bed, all of the covers and both pillows. She was facedown, sprawled out and dead to the world.

Since he risked falling off the bed if he so much as moved, he didn't. He just lay there and looked at her.

Always, he left a woman's bed before the sun came up. So he stared at Emma, waiting for the claustrophobia to overcome him.

Nothing.

Still, he waited, for it would happen. It always did. It was why he wanted out of his "Hollywood" lifestyle, wanted to meet the kind of woman he could wake up with and feel excited about instead of panicked.

In anticipation of the need to run, he forced himself to slip out of bed. Leaning over her, he kissed her lightly before backing to the door.

He always left, he reminded himself. And he was

leaving now because they had no future. He was leaving now because she'd wanted only one night.

He was leaving now for the biggest reason of all.

Because he didn't want to.

He looked down at her, sleeping so deeply. If she moved, if she so much as twitched, he would stay.

But she didn't.

THE NINTH PHOTO SHOOT was two days later. Emma had agonized over it for most of that time. She had agonized over everything since the moment she'd woken up alone in her bed the night after Rafe had—

Well. Thinking about what Rafe had done to her that night brought both the memory of incredible pleasure—more than she'd ever known—and a good amount of pain.

Because that was the night she'd realized she was in trouble when it came to her feelings about Rafe Delacantro. Maybe she'd realized it before then, but it hadn't been until he'd made love to her, in her bed, in her shower, on the kitchen table at three in the morning while they were feeding each other cheese and crackers, that she'd been able to face it. She was in deep.

So much for keeping a clear head about this.

Now, hours before the shoot, Amber sat on Emma's bed, munching on yogurt, her idea of junk food. Emma's idea of junk food was a big old bag of chips. Thank God for good metabolism.

"Are you sure?" Amber asked for the fifth time as Emma stared at herself in the mirror. "Because, quite honestly, I don't get why you have to do this."

"I know." Emma didn't know how to put into words why she wanted to do this shoot instead of having Amber do it. She figured it was a sneaky way of seeing Rafe again, since she knew the way he'd left the other morning without waking her up meant that either she'd completely disappointed him or he was scared of his feelings for her in the same way she was scared of her feelings for him.

But she couldn't imagine Rafe scared of anything.

Which meant she'd disappointed him.

Hard on the ego, but she'd had two long nights to agonize over it now. She could have been more aggressive, hotter, more earthy somehow—she just knew it. Maybe she could convince him to come back out to her place tonight and they'd try again—

"Because if I didn't know better," Amber said carefully, "I'd guess you were really into him. But since I do know better, it has to be something else, right?"

Emma pulled on her ear. "Right."

"Ha!" Amber leaped off the bed and pointed at her. "You're lying! You always pull on your ear when you're lying. You're into him, you really are. I knew it. Damn, Emma. Not Rafe. Anyone but Rafe."

"Well, I—"

"I told you, he's not the man to mess around with."

"Look who's talking. You're messing around with his best friend."

"But we've both been around the block and have no illusions. We know how to mess around with our bodies, not our hearts. You don't."

"I'm learning."

"You, the prude, the Goodie Two-shoes, can sleep with him and get it out of your system?"

"Yes. In fact, I've already washed him right out of my system, thank you very much."

"And that's that."

"And that's that," Emma confirmed.

Amber's eyes narrowed. "So why are you doing this shoot?"

Good question. "I told you, I have a secret Harley-Davidson fantasy. I want to wear leather and lie over a motorcycle and have every guy's tongue hang out."

Amber didn't look convinced. "Really?"

Emma mentally crossed her fingers. "Really. Don't take this experience away from me."

"You're crazy, you know that?"

Yep. She knew that.

THEY DID THE HARLEY SHOOT at night, with the moon and stars as their backdrop on Mulholland Drive overlooking L.A. far below.

Rafe mostly watched, letting Stone handle all the crucial decisions on the setup. He knew Stone loved this business with all his heart, and he also knew his friend would do as well or better than Rafe had. He had the patience and temperament for it.

More power to him.

They were waiting for Jen to bring their model to the top of the hill for the shoot. "It won't be Emma," Stone said with certainty, when they were all set up. "I talked to Amber, and she said—"

"You talked to Amber?"

"Yeah."

"You hate to talk to Amber."

"I don't hate looking at her."

"Or sleeping with her?"

Stone lifted a shoulder. "She's not quite as certifiable as I thought she was."

"You have a thing for her."

"I wouldn't talk if I were you. You have a thing for her twin."

Rafe stared at him, then sighed. "It's a sad, sad day when the two of *us* are hooked."

"I'm not hooked," Stone said. "Not even close."

"Yeah. Me, neither."

Much.

When the car carrying the model arrived, they were ready for her. A long, leather-clad leg emerged, followed by a torso covered with a leather push-up bra.

Rafe swallowed hard while he waited for the face to emerge and look at him. Stone had told him it would be Amber. She was ready to work and wanted to work—two separate things with Amber—so he truly expected Emma's twin to be the one sprawling across the big bike for his camera.

And that was for the best, anyway. He hadn't talked to Emma since their night together. He'd figured each of them would be best served by a little distance. If what they'd each said was true and this was just a physical release, then it should be over.

And maybe if that *had* been true, he would have been able to sleep for the past two nights, without waking up feeling as though he was missing something. The best something.

The model turned and faced them and when he saw her eyes he didn't know whether to laugh or cry.

She walked right up to him, keeping her gaze on his the entire time. "Hey."

"Hey, yourself."

"Ready to do this?"

"Are you?" he asked.

"Where do you want me?" she asked instead of answering.

He pointed to the bike, and she moved that way, a vision in the hip-hugging, incredibly low-riding leather pants.

"Straddle it."

Lifting a leg, Emma straddled the bike and tossed back her hair so it tumbled down her nearly bare back. She sent him a look over her shoulder, turning her body to best emphasize her full breasts and how the leather bra was barely containing them. If she moved another fraction, nipples were going to pop out. Sitting, her pants sank even lower on her hips, and he could see the line of her black lace thong coming out the top, the strings skimming her hips. He had no idea what it was about the top of a thong peeking out like that, but it got him and got him good.

"How's this?" she asked silkily.

Just about perfect. Since no sound came out, he cleared his throat. "Good."

Stone handed him his camera with a long look in his eyes that said "I haven't a clue why she's here any more than you do," and backed away to let Rafe get the shot.

He directed her to a few different poses, many of which had her sitting on the bike sideways, facing the camera, with one leg up and bent, her heel close to her crotch as she smiled saucily. He took a shot, but his mind was convinced that he could clearly see the outline of her nipples—impossible through the leather. And in the V of her tight leather pants, he was sure he could see the outline of her most feminine, intimate place. A place he'd been and touched and kissed and sucked—

He lowered the camera. He couldn't do it, he couldn't take a picture of her like that and let unknown men drool over it.

With a deep breath, he called, "Finished."

"That's it?" Stone came up behind him. "You sure you shot enough film, because—"

"I got enough." And if he didn't, he'd improvise. "We're done here."

Stone slowly shook his head. "It's a wrap," he called out to the crew and then, for Rafe's ears alone, he said, "You've lost it."

Organized chaos ensued as the crew moved out. Rafe walked up to Emma.

"Some fantasy, huh?" she said softly, running her hands down her leather pants. "I've never worn anything like it." She let out a startlingly alluring smile tinged with shyness. "I liked it."

God, she was something. Beautiful. Sexy. Adorable. And he wanted, quite badly, to haul her into his arms and tell her what he liked, which was her naked, in bed, panting his name.

"Want to continue the fantasy?"

She looked startled. "What do you mean?"

"I mean, let's take the bike out."

"Are you sure?"

"Oh, yeah." He lifted the keys from his pocket. "It's a friend's. Come on." He had no idea why he was coaxing her into this. Maybe to drive himself a little more crazy.

Or maybe to see if she was just as crazy.

Either way, she waited for him, waited while the crew finished cleaning up, waited until they were alone on top of the world.

He got on the bike and handed her the helmet. The engine roared to life as she climbed on behind him.

She plastered her long, willowy body to his, wrapped her arms around his waist, and pressed her lush breasts into his back.

He drove her into the night, with the wind in their faces, with the stars and the moon for light, with nothing for music but the wild beating of his heart—and hers, which he could feel palpitating against his back.

The dark, curvy roads were perfect for his mood and he leaned into each turn, loving how her arms felt surrounding him, loving how she settled her chin on his shoulder to see. He could turn his head, look into her smiling eyes and know she was enjoying this every bit as much as he was.

Eventually they landed back at the same spot on the top of Mulholland Drive. He braced the bike upright with one leg, feeling her body lean into his trustingly, warm and pliant.

"So," she said softly.

"So."

"Only three shots left."

"Yep."

"Had any luck enjoying your impending retirement?" she asked.

He stared down into the city lights and let out a small laugh. "I bought a plant."

"A plant."

"A houseplant. I'll actually be around to water it."

"Ah." She nodded. "That sounds...domestic."

"One houseplant sounds domestic?"

“I don’t have any plants,” she said quietly. “I work too much and forget to water them.”

“That’s you.”

She was silent for a moment, then nodded. “Yeah. That’s me.” She sighed. “So what else? There’s Puddles, right?”

“I wanted a puppy,” he said. “And I ended up with a crotchety cat.”

She was quiet for so long that he craned his neck to look at her. “What?”

“I’d forget to feed a cat, too.” She shook her head. “I hate that about myself.” In a gesture that was as slight as it was telling, she pulled away from him. “I’d better get home. I have a long day at work tomorrow.”

He’d been hoping for something else from her entirely, but he wasn’t sure what. Another long, incredibly sensual night? How could he want that when she wasn’t what he wanted at all?

He didn’t know, but he did.

But he still just drove her home.

18

EMMA ENDED UP SPENDING much of the week at the studio, as they were working up storyboards for the next six months' worth of plots. Normally she didn't have much planning control, but in the past few weeks she'd really delivered in the wild-and-sexy department, and the "suits" were feeling generous.

And, quite frankly, they were curious as well, wanting to see what she could come up with next. She had lots of scenarios planned in her head, using such props as a pool or a Harley-Davidson, and maybe even a trip to the islands. Just thinking about it made her grin.

And ache.

Because she doubted she'd ever forget how she'd gotten such ideas or the man who'd given them to her. She hadn't heard from him and she knew that was her own fault. She'd pushed him away.

Funny thing, though—during the long hours, surrounded by suits and the director and the other writers, all of whom lived and breathed this soap opera world, suddenly she couldn't remember why she did.

Why did she work around the clock for a television

show? Was it the respect and love of her peers? No. Was it the money? A resounding no.

So why?

She had the terrible feeling that maybe, just maybe, it was because she had nothing else in her life, so she relied on work.

On Monday, there was a crisis. One of their favorite female leads wanted out of her contract to take a movie deal, and everyone was up in arms. Emma took it in stride. No biggie, they could kill her off.

On Tuesday, one of their teen males fell off his bike and broke both legs. Again everyone fell apart. Emma offered to write him into a coma.

On Wednesday, the union grumbled about a strike. On Thursday, an hour of film was lost. By Friday, the place was just about crisis-overloaded.

And yet she felt nothing but the oddest sense of detachment.

On Friday afternoon, it occurred to her that she hadn't heard about any more photo shoots, specifically October and November, which she knew were to take place over the weekend. Thinking that was strange since she usually knew by Thursday what was expected, she wrote herself a note to call Amber that night.

And she refused to let herself dwell on the fact that the reason she felt so curious was that she knew she had only three excuses left to see Rafe.

Just as she thought that, Amber entered her office wearing a hot-pink sundress and a grin. ''Hey, sis.''

''Hey. I was just thinking about you, wondering if you've heard anything about this weekend's photo shoot.''

''Yep.'' She plopped into the chair, tossed back her mane of hair and revealed a hickey on her neck.

''New boyfriend?''

Amber laughed. ''Stone.''

''I thought he was a one-time thing.''

''Make that a two-time thing— Nope, scratch that, it's been three times now.'' Amber waggled her eyebrows. ''And talented as he is, I'm thinking of make it four, just for fun.''

''The shoot,'' Emma said, not wanting to hear details about her sister and Stone. ''What have you heard about the shoot?''

''It went fabulously.''

Emma blinked. ''Went? As in past tense?''

''They called the other day, and I couldn't reach you. For October we did a bubble bath scene, and then we shot November right afterward. I had a choice this time of costume. Can you believe that Stone let me pick? A red or black negligee on this cool bedroom set. I chose the black because it sets off my tan so nicely. And Rafe finished in less than hour, so I must be getting even better than I thought. There's only one shot left now, tonight in Malibu. Anyway—'' she hopped up ''—just wanted to tell you the good news.''

Emma couldn't think past the fact that she'd just lost two of three chances to be with Rafe. "Good news?"

Amber tried to look cool but couldn't contain her grin. "I got a part on a pilot for the fall schedule. It's a comedy." She let out a little scream of joy. "Can you believe it?"

"Amber, that's...amazing." Emma laughed and hugged her sister tight. "I'm so happy for you."

"I know, I am, too. And given how generous I'm feeling, I think Stone just might get lucky for that fourth time soon. Maybe even tonight." She danced toward the door. "I think I'll just go out to Frederick's of Hollywood and find something suitably outrageous to wear under my dress. Come with?"

Emma thought of the work she had left to do and shook her head.

"You know, I'll never understand why you do what you do when it takes all of your time. Look at me—I make a lot more money than you do, and I have at least twice the spare time. You work too hard, Emma."

"Yes, I know. I—" But she had to laugh, because Amber was already gone.

Emma got back to work but couldn't concentrate. She kept picturing herself in the negligee Amber hadn't chosen—the red one—posing for Rafe.

RAFE LAY ON A FLOAT in his pool, letting the sun bake him while the cool water lapped at his body. Only one shoot left, and all the prep work was complete. After years of working night and day, lying here on a week-day with nothing claiming his time felt incredibly decadent.

"Meow."

Peering out of one eye, he took in the cat sitting a good three feet back from the edge of the pool, watching him with distaste. "Go do what you do. Nap or something."

"Meow."

Ah, hell. He drifted over to the edge. "All right. Come on over here."

The cat eyed the water and lifted her nose.

He waggled his fingers, and with a sigh that said she was clearly queen and simply humoring him, she came a little closer, just enough that he could reach up and scratch her beneath that raised chin.

Immediately her eyes closed and a rumble came from her chest. She purred all the time now, and slept on his feet at night so that he couldn't even feel them when he woke up in the morning.

He'd always dreamed of a puppy, a big, sloppy one that would show him affection and blind devotion. "But somehow," he murmured, "you work, too."

As if tired of his pampering, she simply turned away, tail raised to the sky, paws practically pointed as she strutted off as if she could no longer be bothered.

What could he do but laugh?

''Great, you've gone to the loony bin already and you haven't even officially stopped working yet.'' Stone, who'd apparently let himself in, dove into the pool. Surfacing near Rafe, he sighed with pleasure. ''Man, that felt good. I'm done in the darkroom with those last two shoots.''

Those last two were still a sore subject for Rafe. They hadn't been with Emma, and when he'd realized he had Amber standing in front of him in a black negligee, he'd gone in one heartbeat from taut anticipation to a frustrated edginess.

Amber had been surprisingly helpful and relatively quiet as well, letting him do his thing in a timely fashion. She'd actually wanted to please them. ''Them'' being mostly Stone, but Rafe appreciated it, nonetheless.

He was afraid he was never going to see Emma again.

''Did they come out okay?'' he asked Stone now.

''Just as good as the others. Impossible to tell we have used two entirely different models.''

He'd be able to tell. Why hadn't Emma come? He could have seen her in that red negligee—somehow the red would have suited her better than the black Amber had picked.

''You could call her, you know,'' Stone said, flopping over in the water to float on his back.

''Who?''

"Who?" He laughed. "Emma, who."

"I don't need to call her."

"Why can't you just admit you fell for her? So she isn't Martha Stewart, big deal."

"I'm not looking for Martha Stewart."

"Really? What are you looking for?" Stone rolled his eyes when Rafe didn't—couldn't—reply, and dove under the water to swim laps.

Leaving Rafe with only his own doubts for company.

THAT EVENING, Emma decided she'd had enough. She'd been working nonstop for days, running on caffeine and little sleep.

She sat in a meeting surrounded by suits, bleary-eyed, feeling as if she'd let her life pass her by.

She knew they'd be here all weekend, and for the first time in…well, ever, she had somewhere else she wanted to be.

A photo shoot in the Malibu hills. It wasn't a sudden urge to be a model that drove her. In fact, after this fantasy calendar shoot was over, she intended to never be in front of camera again.

Nope, what drove her was the need to see this thing through with Rafe. She hadn't expected her desire for him to increase with each passing day and she certainly hadn't expected that desire to be more than physical.

But the physical want alone was going to kill her.

She needed him.

She wondered if he felt the same. She had to know. She put her hands on the table and rose.

Everyone looked at her in surprise.

"I'm out of here," she said.

"What?" Several suits said this in unison, staring at her as if she'd grown wings.

Maybe she had.

"I think my eighty hours so far this week is sufficient."

"But…" The executive producer blinked. "We're not done."

"I know, but I am." Gently, because they all looked confused, and really, she would have felt the same way not too long ago, she stopped to explain. "I need a little break."

"But we still have to get your pages for—"

"You'll have them. I'll e-mail them later tonight."

"But you never need a break," said a shocked producer.

"I know." But she needed one now.

THE HILLS OF MALIBU were still warm and beautiful when Emma arrived for the shoot. She pulled into the driveway of the house that had been rented for its private beach, and thought maybe she should use this location for her show, too.

She wondered what Rafe would say when he saw

her. Would his eyes light up, would he toss her that slow, sexy-as-hell grin that weakened her knees?

To her shock, this shoot was already under way. At the back of the house, wearing a sunshine-yellow one-piece swimsuit and lit by the stars, the moon and a few strategic spotlights, stood her sister, modeling on the deck. Emma couldn't hear the words of the photographer, who kneeled with his back to her, but she didn't have to. She remembered exactly how his low, raspy voice sounded, how arousing his softly uttered directions were, how the silky nuances made her want to give him whatever he asked for. She looked at the way his shirt stretched taut over broad, sleek muscles and wondered if he still bore the marks of her fingernails.

And then Amber tossed her head back at something he said, laughing like she didn't have a care in the world.

"Tough to watch, isn't it?"

In surprise, Emma turned and found Stone standing there, looking at her with a mixture of sympathy and mutual misery. "What?"

"I know what you're going through. The unreasonable jealousy."

Emma tried to laugh, but it stuck in her throat. "It's so stupid."

"I know." Stone watched as Amber pulled and adjusted her costume until her breasts nearly popped out of the suit. Then she turned her back to the camera, revealing how high she'd pulled up the thong back, which allowed them to see…just about everything.

Stone's jaw bunched and jumped. "Excuse me," he said to Emma. "Hold it!" he called out to Rafe and Amber, both of whom turned in surprise. "The wind is getting too fierce. Let's wrap."

Rafe glanced around in bafflement. "What?"

"It's windy, Rafe," Stone said, and, striding forward, he grabbed a white fluffy robe from Jen's hands and flung it around Amber's shoulders. "Far too windy to work."

He waved away Jen and another assistant, instead leading Amber himself. As he did, Emma heard Amber say, "What the hell is wrong with you?"

"What the hell is wrong with me?" Stone asked with a harsh laugh. "I'll tell you what the hell is wrong with me. I just learned something about myself."

"Yeah? What's that—that you're an ass?"

"No." Stone's jaw tensed further. "That I don't like you showing off for everyone. I want you to only show it off for me."

Amber stumbled and might have fallen if Stone hadn't been holding her up. She stopped and stared at him. "What? What did you just say?"

Instead of answering, Stone hauled her up to her toes and kissed her—kissed her hard and deep, by the looks of it.

Emma winced for him, expecting Amber to step

back and slap him, maybe even drop-kick him to the ground, but instead Amber clung to him for more.

When Stone pulled back, chest heaving, eyes dark, he said, "I hate what you do. I hate that you always take jobs that require so little clothing."

Amber let out a surprised laugh and put her hand to her mouth. "My God. It's more than sex. You really like me."

Stone blew out a breath. "Yeah. Guess I do."

"Well, guess what?"

Stone looked wary. "What?"

"I like you back. And guess what else?"

"I'm feeling a little weak, Amber. Maybe you could just tell me."

She beamed. "I just got a comedy pilot for TV."

"A comedy?"

"Yep. Know what that means? No more stripping. I get to keep my clothes on from now on."

Stone hauled her back into his arms. "Except with me," he growled, and he kissed her again. Then he led her away.

In shock, Emma watched them go. She couldn't believe what had just happened. A man had tamed her sister. A nice man. A normal man.

Emma was thrilled for Amber. She was also…sad. She wanted that. She wanted what Amber had managed to find for herself.

A man to want her, a man to want her for keeps.

She had let work take precedence, so much so that

she'd pushed away all the men who might have been interested. She was consumed and too much of a perfectionist.

But even *she* knew those weren't the only reasons she was alone.

The truth was, she'd never been interested enough to have a man hang around. Until now.

She was interested now, and in only one man.

Then she looked up and found that one man.

19

ALL RAFE HAD WANTED TO DO was get the shot finished and be done. Yes, he would rather have worked with Emma, but it had been Amber's gig from the beginning and there was nothing he could do about that.

Emma wasn't in his world—neither the world he was leaving nor the world he was heading toward.

And yet, there she stood, alone and quiet, watching him.

He felt a little unnerved to find her looking at him as though someone had shot her puppy, so he moved around the equipment that an assistant was putting away and walked toward her.

She didn't run, but she looked as if she might be on the verge. She looked unsure and unhappy, and his heart cracked as he gazed at her.

Having no idea what he would say, he kept moving toward her.

Her eyes were huge, her fingers clasped together, and, as she did when she felt unsettled, she was nibbling on her lower lip. He wondered, Did she feel any of what he did? How could she not?

One thing he could see was the fear beneath the nerves, and he understood that all too well. With a hope that was startlingly intense, he increased his pace, and when he was about ten feet from her she did something not so surprising.

She whirled and ran. She bunched up her skirt a little in her fists, hitting the sand running, her peasant-style blouse fluttering around her torso, her long flowing skirt brushing her calves and knees.

"Emma, wait!"

When she didn't, he whirled back to the assistant and Jen, both of whom were watching the second show in as many minutes, looking utterly captivated. "Jen—"

She lifted a hand toward the equipment. "I've got it."

Knowing he could leave the expensive camera and equipment without worry, he started after Emma.

This part of Malibu was all private beach, but there were also jagged rocks and bluffs that made it impossible to see more than the immediate stretch of sand before him. Following Emma around one rock larger than his entire garage, he found himself in a small cove, completely buffeted from view by the bluffs.

Emma stood right at the water's edge, her back to him, her shoulders heaving with exertion with each breath.

"Emma."

Her shoulders stiffened, but she didn't turn toward him.

"The crew is going to be talking about tonight for a while to come," he said.

"I didn't meant to make things difficult for you."

"You know I don't care about that."

Bending, she picked up a rock and chucked it as far into the pounding waves as she could, shielding her eyes against the moon's glow to try to see the rock as it hit.

"Why did you run?"

She picked up another rock. "Because I'm a writer who can't seem to articulate her feelings."

For a man used to provoking feelings in people with his work, he hadn't done such a great job articulating his, either. "What's going on, Emma?"

She reached for another rock. "I'm happy for Amber. For the first time in her life, she's in a good place. She's got a job she actually wants and a man to boot, one who will be good for her for a change."

Sensing her loneliness, maybe because it matched his, he moved up behind her. A strand of her hair whipped in the wind, catching on his jaw. Her skirt entwined in his legs, making them feel as if they were touching even though they weren't.

"So you're happy for Amber. That's why you ran."

"I ran because I had all these strange feelings rushing through me, with jealousy leading the pack, and I didn't like what that said about me. And then I looked up and saw you, and..."

"And...?" Though she had Don't Touch signs all over her, starting with her stiff shoulders and the way she still hadn't turned to look at him, he lifted his hand and stroked her arm, stroked up and down, and then entwined their fingers.

"And I wanted you," she whispered, squeezing his fingers. "I wanted you to follow me."

"For sex on the beach?"

After a slight pause, in which he held his breath and his heart didn't beat, she nodded.

"Yes."

He felt a flash of disappointment, because for that one moment in time, he'd wanted to hear something else entirely. He turned her toward him, shocked to find her eyes swimming in tears.

"Hey," he said softly, and he cupped her face. A teardrop hit his thumb. "What's this?"

She shook her head and slowly wrapped her arms around his neck, pressing her mouth to his. "I don't want to talk," she murmured. "I want to feel." Tossing back her head to study the sky, exposing her slim throat and thrusting her breasts to his chest, she said, "It's a beautiful, glorious night and I don't want to be alone." Then she looked at him with her soul in her eyes, breaking his heart. "Tell me you still want me."

He stared at her, into her beautiful, wet eyes, into the face he dreamed about, at the body he wanted more than anything. "Yes. Yes, I still want you, but—"

She put her fingers to his lips and then slowly ran them over the sensitive flesh, back and forth, her eyes dark and promising. "No buts."

Right. No regrets, no overthinking… Just living for the moment, at least when it came to this woman. He dragged his mouth down her throat, nibbling, tasting, licking, absorbing her gasp of pleasure.

She sank her fingers into his hair, holding his head close as he worked his way over her collarbone and toward a breast. "Yes."

They sank to their knees in the sand. She needed, he needed, and beneath the glorious midnight sky, they were going to fulfill those needs. Even as a small part of her realized this was only a momentary fix for the strange and inexplicable…loneliness coursing through her, she didn't care.

Because Rafe kissed like heaven. He tasted like heaven.

He made her feel as though she was in heaven.

The cove was protected and extremely private. No one else could access it, except through the house they'd rented for the shoot, but so great was her hunger for him that shamelessly, she didn't even care.

He pulled his shirt over his head, laid it out behind her and then followed her down.

There was something about the soft, giving, still-warm sand beneath her and Rafe's hard but giving body above her. She nearly cried out in pleasure from the contact. Pulling his head to hers, she kissed him, kissed him long and deep and hard, kissed him until all her thoughts scattered like the wind around them.

Bracing his weight on his elbows, he framed her face with his hands, sweeping her hair out of their way. ''You're so beautiful, Emma.'' As if painting a picture, he ran a finger lightly over her lips; her jaw, her throat, her shoulder, until her entire body throbbed for his touch.

And then he slipped off her onto his side. ''I'm not going anywhere,'' he promised when she murmured a protest, continuing his exploration of her body with his fingers.

She arched up, ran her hands up his arms, over his chest. ''Rafe. Hurry.''

''Getting there.'' Unbuttoning her blouse, he spread the material wide and then did the same to her front-clasp bra, baring her to the dark night and his equally dark gaze. Cupping a breast, he teased the tip with his thumb, coaxing a thready moan from her throat just before he bent to suck her into his mouth.

Sliding her fingers through his hair, she held his head close to her body, tossing back her own. Above her the stars glowed, while Rafe made her body do the same. His fingers danced down her quivering belly, then slowly bunched up her skirt, baring first her lower legs and then her thighs, all while his mouth continued to suck and nibble at her breasts. His tongue laved over the very tip, over and around, and then he used his teeth, lightly scraping her sensitized flesh until she could hardly stand it.

His fingers skimmed up past her panties now, so that she felt the cool night on her belly. He ran his fingers over the silk of her panties.

Her legs fell open for him.

His fingers took advantage of that, tracing her right down the center and then slowly back up, this time slipping beneath the silk. His knuckles grazed her bare flesh, ripping a shockingly needy sound from her throat.

At that, he set his big hand on her inner thigh and urged her legs open even farther, then gripped the crotch of her panties in his hand, dragging them aside enough to fully expose her to the night air.

He tore his mouth away from her breast to look down at what he'd done, letting out a rough groan. "This I've got to have." And he leaned over her, kissing first one inner thigh and then the other, and then right in between. She gasped his name and arched up.

"Perfect," he murmured, and he lowered his head again, gently outlining her with his tongue.

Beyond rational thought now, she fisted her hands in his shirt at her sides and let him take her.

And take her he did. He used his tongue, he used his teeth, he used his fingers as well, and she thrashed beneath him, finally reaching for the zipper on his pants, needing him inside her.

"Come first," he whispered, holding her off. "Stop holding back and come for me, Emma."

"I'm not."

But actually, she was, if only because a small part of her was so afraid this wasn't going to be enough, that she could have sex with him every night of the week and it wouldn't ever be enough…

Surging up, he lay at her side and pressed his mouth just beneath her ear. "I'm not going anywhere." As he said this, he slid a long finger into her.

She stifled a cry. "Rafe."

"That's right, just me." He added another finger as he used his teeth lightly on her throat, bathing the little love bites with his tongue. "The man who wants to drive you out of your mind tonight beneath these stars. Go crazy for me, show me everything. Let it all go." His fingers eased in, then pulled out, while his thumb worked magic on the spot designed for his touch. In and out. More thumb. In and out.

The anticipation came from so deep down that she didn't know how to turn away from it. Desperation had her gripping his wrist, holding him in place, even though he crooned softly in her ear, wordless little murmurs that promised he was staying where he was.

"Emma." His thumb circled again, and she whimpered an inarticulate answer. "Come for me…"

It started in her toes, the shudder that ripped through her, the cry that tore through her lungs and burst out of her as she did just that.

She lost some time then, maybe a moment, maybe more, as she drifted slowly back to her senses. She heard him tear open a condom and forced her eyes open, just in time to watch him roll it down the length of him. There was something incredibly sensual about seeing his hands on himself, and then even more when he sank into her.

"Oh," she breathed in wonder as her body began to tighten again. "Rafe..."

"Yeah. Again," he demanded, eyes narrowed, face fierce with concentration as he began to move.

She left her eyes open, though it was a struggle, watched his emotions chase one another across his face as he pistoned his hips against hers, taking her to a place she'd never been before, to a place she'd never known existed.

EMMA DRIFTED AWAKE to find herself cradled against Rafe's warm body, the cool night air drifting over them, his fingers lightly stroking her arm.

"Hmm," she sighed. Then her eyes flew wide open and she sat all the way up. "I can't believe I fell asleep."

"Only for a moment." He sat up and swept a strand of hair out of her face. "You're tired."

Extremely. She'd been working too hard, and thinking even harder, so sleep had been difficult, but—

"Come back to my house with me," he said. "We can just go to sleep or watch a late movie, whatever you want to do."

Go back to his place... That would be lovely. If she hadn't promised to have her pages done. "I'm sorry, but—"

"But you have work."

"Only a bit."

For a few moments he lay there looking up at her. Then in one fluid motion he got to his feet. He was still shirtless, and his temper was all the more magnificent for it.

"That's all right, Emma. You go back to your work."

"I will," she said quietly. "But I'll be done by—"

He lifted a hand. "No explanation required. I don't need an excuse."

"I'm not trying to excuse anything," she said tightly. "I'm just trying to tell you I can come back."

"Don't worry about it. I get that you live for your work. I get it loud and clear. So go on, go back to it, go back to your boring, workaholic life."

She could only stare at him, at a complete loss in the face of his anger.

"Go on," he said, and he waggled his fingers for her to go.

Well, damn him, anyway. Maybe she *was* a workaholic, but she sure as hell didn't need him to throw it in her face. To make it sound like it was awful and horrible and...boring.

"Goodbye, Rafe."

He turned away, shoved his hands in his pockets.

And without another word, she walked away.

20

AFTER THAT NIGHT, Emma worked like a demon. The studio didn't protest, they loved it. Two weeks into her mad-woman writing schedule, they gave her a bonus and offered to renegotiate her contract, saying the pages she'd been giving them were her best ever. Emmy-award winning, they all vowed.

She read between the lines with the best of them. They wanted to guarantee that she kept up the pace yet didn't get lured away by another show.

But after another week of the grueling schedule, with her eyes perpetually red and strained, her body falling apart, her nails chewed down to the nubs, she wondered what it was about her that she found it so impossible to change.

She'd wanted something different, something more. Even Amber had managed to get that something more. In addition to her new TV pilot, she had a man in her life, a real man.

Emma sighed. What made that all so hard for her?

She had one meeting left for the day. The studio was going to hire another junior writer and, as part of the interview process, wannabe scribes would come in one at a time and pitch their ideas.

After that, she could go home to bed.

Grabbing a large coffee for the meeting, which promised to be long and excruciating, she glanced at her reflection in the glass. Her hair was piled on top of her head and held there precariously with two pencils. She wore leggings and a large T-shirt. Amber wouldn't have been caught dead looking like this.

She looked about as different from the model she'd pretended to be as she could get.

Entering the conference room, she slouched down in a chair, thinking no one outside this place would recognize her, not her sister, not Rafe—

Nope, she thought as her heart constricted without permission, *I'm not going to go there.* To make sure she didn't, she dove into the tray of cookies in the middle of the conference table. Boring? Is that what he'd said her life was? Ha! This wasn't boring. She grabbed another cookie.

Chocolate always had been able to solve everything. Today she was going to put it to the test.

"YOU'RE...WHAT?" Stone stared at Rafe in disbelief. He'd just shown up at Rafe's house, wearing a damn shit-eating grin that assured Rafe his best friend had been getting lucky on a regular basis.

He intended to get lucky himself. He hadn't slept well for weeks, until last night. "I'm going after her."

"You're going after her." Stone blinked. "Emma? Hollywood writer, workaholic Emma?"

"Yep." He stepped outside, pulled Stone out as well, and locked his front door.

Stone, mouth hanging open, watched Rafe walk past him toward his car. "You're going to get Emma."

"You're sounding a bit like a parrot."

"But..." Stone looked confused. "I thought she wasn't the one."

"I was wrong."

"So what are you going to do, kidnap her from work?"

"I'm going to try something new."

"What's that?"

"I'm going to tell her how I feel."

"Oh." Stone thought about that for a moment, then nodded. "It was a new technique for me, as well."

"And it worked for you," Rafe pointed out.

"It sure did."

"Then, wish me luck."

"Good luck."

"Thanks."

"You're going to need it," Stone added.

THEY'D HEARD SO MANY PITCHES, Emma's head was going to explode. No one writer had stood out, and they were beginning to think the entire process was going to be a wash.

Emma still sat at the conference table. Her mug had

been filled over and over and, as a result, she felt jittery. Maybe it had been the cookies and caffeine and no lunch, but her head hurt and she wanted a nap.

She rested her head on the table. "Let's send whoever's left out there home. It's not worth it."

"A few more," someone else decided and yelled "Next!" to the assistant standing by the door.

Emma lifted her head just as a tall, dark and heart-stoppingly handsome man walked into the room.

Rafe.

"Hello," he said in a hauntingly familiar voice. He lifted the clipboard he held. "I'm here to pitch a concept."

"Go ahead," said the suit on Emma's left.

Emma sat there with her mouth open. What was he doing? Why was he here? And why, oh why, did he have to look so…kissable? She'd done her best to get over him. She'd done her best not to think about him every living, breathing second. She'd nearly succeeded, too. In fact, she hadn't thought about him in at least four whole minutes.

And now here he was, in the flesh, looking at her with so much emotion in his eyes she could hardly stand it. *What is he doing?*

Rafe cleared his throat and, instead of reading from a paper as everyone else had done, put his clipboard behind his back and looked right at her. "My concept is simple. It's a relationship concept."

Oh God.

"What I'm envisioning," he said, "is a man and a woman, in the perpetual struggle to find not only themselves, but love."

Around her, a few suits nodded, interested.

Emma could hardly breathe. She didn't know what the hell he thought he was doing, but she couldn't take it. She just couldn't—

"It opens with a man," Rafe said. "He has his heart set on breaking free from his too-busy, too-hectic, too-controlled lifestyle. He wants to settle down away from all that. He wants to, for once, have the time to indulge in an affair of the heart."

His eyes were on Emma, and she slowly became aware that everyone else's were, too. She glanced around and tried to looked nonplussed, while her pulse beat unnaturally fast and heavy.

Even when she didn't look at him, she could feel Rafe's eyes on her, pulling, capturing, holding, and she made the mistake of turning back to him.

A mistake because now she couldn't tear her gaze off him.

Rafe took a breath and went on. "But the love of his life is also in that crazy, too-hectic, too-controlled lifestyle," Rafe said. "She doesn't realize how much of herself she gives, leaving nothing for anything else. Or anyone else. This breaks the man's heart, because he wants her to see him, to be with him. To plant flowers in the yard and raise a grumpy old cat together."

"Maybe he should find someone else," Emma said.

"Maybe he doesn't want to."

"Maybe she can't be who he wants," she said.

"Maybe she's wrong."

All eyes in the room volleyed back and forth between the two of them.

"Maybe the only woman he wants is her," Rafe said. "You," he clarified softly.

Their observers gasped in concert.

Emma's heart went to her throat.

"In my concept, this man has said a few things in frustration, things he didn't really mean," he said. "Her life isn't boring or staid, it's just different from his—and he's incredibly sorry."

"You don't have to—"

"I should never have said those things, Emma."

At the use of her name, everyone again turned toward her. She felt her face heat up.

"This is a concept, not real life."

"Right." But he looked disappointed at having to keep up the pretense. "In my *concept,* these two see each other, they go out, they spend lots of time together, despite all their differences, despite all the things they've said to each other, or not said. In my concept," he added softly, "they work hard. But a relationship, a good one, is worth the hard work."

Emma closed her eyes. She felt so confused. Still hurt. And afraid, terribly afraid, that he'd change his mind. That he couldn't possibly really want her. She couldn't handle that, couldn't handle jumping in, giving him everything, only to find out he didn't mean it. She didn't have good luck with people being there for her.

"I'm sorry," she said, looking at him through a veil of tears she refused to let fall. "But we're not interested."

She could feel the stare of every one of her peers, silent, sad, probably thinking she'd just made a huge mistake.

But it was her mistake to make, damn it. "You can go."

"Emma—"

"Please," she whispered, covering her eyes.

It wasn't until she heard the conference door close behind him that she opened her eyes and took a breath.

He had left. He really had left.

Everyone stared at her.

"Well." She managed a smile. "Is there anyone else?"

"You let him go." The producer across from her, Liz, couldn't seem to get over this. "You let that gorgeous hunk of a man walk right out that door."

"There are extenuating circumstances," she said, hating every one of those extenuating circumstances.

"Honey, he just laid his heart bare in front of a crowd of people, and all for you. I would say screw the circumstances and go after him."

Emma looked at her.

She nodded. "Yep. Drag that man straight home and never let him get away."

Emma turned to stare at the closed conference door, knowing she'd never forget the look on Rafe's face when she'd said she wasn't interested. "I don't think I can keep a man like that."

"Why not?"

Yeah, why not?

Didn't she deserve to have some happiness and joy?

She looked around at the expectant faces, some of whom nodded encouragingly. "I..." She closed her eyes. "I'm an idiot." She leaped up. "I have to go after him."

"Good girl," her producer said.

She raced to the door, then looked back. "I should tell you, I want to cut back."

"Cut back...what?"

Emma smiled, because suddenly this felt like the best idea she'd ever had. "I want to work forty hours a week, not a moment more. I want a life outside of the job. I'll understand if this doesn't work for you, but I love writing soap scripts, so be warned, I'll go to another show if I have to."

"Are you kidding?" asked Liz. "Don't you dare. You just go get that hot man."

Emma hauled open the door. The hallway was crowded with people hustling and bustling around doing their jobs. What she didn't see was a Rafe Delacantro.

She'd catch him in the parking lot. She started to run, grateful for the flat, beat-up sandals she wore. Racing down the hallways, dodging people left and right, tossing out an "I'm sorry" every time she jostled anyone, she skidded out the front glass doors and searched the parking lot.

But he was gone.

21

"MEOW."

"I just fed you," Rafe said to the cat winding its way around his ankles. He wasn't really in the mood. He still couldn't grasp the reality that it was over with Emma, he just couldn't.

Puddles bit his ankle.

"All right, all right. Hold on." He stood in his living room, a few nails in his mouth, his hammer in his hand, surveying the north wall critically. He'd hung a series of his photographs on the bare wall. "What do you think?"

Puddles sat and began to wash her face.

"Thanks."

Irena had asked about the bare walls, saying they definitely needed something. She'd suggested pictures of the celebrities he'd taken shots of over the years, or maybe some of the recognizable places he'd been to. Something to exhibit his work.

He had figured he'd get to it eventually—eventually being later. But tonight, after the day from hell, he'd needed the chore to keep his mind off Emma's rejection.

So he'd taken Irena's suggestion under consideration and decided she was right. He needed stuff on his walls. *His* stuff.

Flipping through his photos had distracted him from thoughts of Emma for a while. He pulled out some of his favorites, remembering trips and people he hadn't thought about in a long time. He'd stayed distracted, a good thing since he didn't seem to enjoy his own company lately.

Today especially.

And man, what a today he'd had, going to Emma's work with his heart in his hands. When he had learned she was unavailable because she was listening to story pitches, he'd gotten that rebrained idea of pitching her a story.

Their story.

She'd listened to him. He knew she had because she'd had trouble breathing. He knew if he'd gone closer, if he'd been able to touch her, she would have been shaking.

He sure as hell had been.

But she'd turned him away.

He looked at the pictures on the wall. They weren't of any famous celebs or anything currently in vogue such as abstract prints. Just his personal favorites, ones he figured he could look at for years to come and never get tired of seeing.

The first two had been taken in Africa. There was one of a lion rolling in complete abandon in a patch of wild grass beneath a blazing summer sun, and another of three village women walking away from the camera, wearing their colorful clothes, with baskets piled high on their heads.

The next few photographs had been taken in Scotland, in the Highlands, far from even a small town. One with the lush green landscape and the ruins of a castle vanishing into a glorious fog, another at midnight during a full moon, the glow highlighting three small huts.

He figured a nice seascape would look good here, and he wondered where he'd take it. Maybe Santa Barbara, during a summer storm—

A knock came at the front door. Puddles, looking unconcerned, continued to wash her face.

"A dog would have warned me someone was coming," he said to her.

She lifted her leg and started in on her private parts.

With a sigh he moved to the door and opened it, figuring it would be Stone or Irena. Maybe one of his sisters. Anyone other than the woman standing there, wearing a sedate blue and white checkered sundress that looked as if it had come from the set of *Leave It to Beaver*.

"It's my housewife costume," said Emma.

"But..." He had to clear his throat because just looking at her made him ache so that he could barely talk. "There's no shoot today. We're...done."

"I know. Can I come in, Rafe?"

Without waiting for an answer, she stepped inside, having to brush against him to do so. His entire body tightened at the feel of her soft skin, and he recognized the scent of her as if he'd already mated for life.

Damn it. Damn *her.* "I'm pretty busy," he said, not wanting to hear about why she'd turned him away earlier. "I'm working."

She made a low tsking sound in her throat as she moved into the living room, studying what he'd put up on the walls. "You know what they say about working too hard." Clasping her hands together, she whirled to face him. "It's not good for you. You don't take time for yourself, to live, to dream. You..." She took a deep breath. "You push people away. People you don't mean to push away."

He looked into her eyes. "Are we talking about me...or you?"

She lifted her hands and brought them to the tiny, neat line of buttons running down the length of her dress. One by one she undid them, and because he was shocked, she got to her belly button before his mouth worked.

"What are you doing?"

With a little shimmy of her shoulders, she allowed the sleeves of the dress to fall to her elbows. Bending slightly, she continued unbuttoning herself. "I was always sorry I didn't get to model this one for you."

Then she straightened. She spread apart the bodice of her dress, revealing that, beneath the modest, housewife outfit, she wore a red silky camisole and matching silky shorts.

He recognized it as the match to the black one that Amber had worn during one of the shoots.

"I'm sorry I rejected your script today," she whispered, dropping the dress entirely, leaving her in only the barely-there red silk. "It was beautiful. It just took a moment to sink in that you could really mean it, that you could really want me for more than just what we shared physically. Then, when I went after you, you were already gone and—"

He stopped her mouth with his, just hauled her close and laid one on her, so overcome with the fact that she was here, that she wanted him, that he could hold her. Only when they needed air did he pull back.

"Rafe—"

"I love you, Emma."

Her breath caught. Her eyes misted. "I wasn't done with my whole spiel. I thought I'd have to sell myself. Promise you that I intend to be less uptight. That I told the studio I was cutting back—"

"There's only one promise I'm wanting."

"Anything," she whispered, holding his hands to her face. "Just ask me."

"Love me back."

Now her eyes overfilled and two drops slipped down, wetting his fingers. "Oh, Rafe." She shot him a tremulous smile. "I do. I love you back. I love you so very, very much." Then she laughed.

"What could possibly be funny?"

"I got off easy." She kissed him, then pulled back, her eyes dancing with love and laughter. "You could have asked me to wear *Leave It to Beaver* dresses every day—"

"God, no." He shuddered.

"Or maybe naughty lingerie—"

"Now *that* works," he said fervently, wrapping his arms around her and lifting her up against him, loving the feel of her creamy skin barely covered in the red silk. He slid his hand beneath those shorts now, his fingers coaxing a gasp out of her. "But with or without the silk, all I want is you. Only you."

"Only you," she vowed back, and tossed her arms around his neck as he scooped her up against him and strode toward his bedroom. "Only you..."

Epilogue

Six months later

AMBER BURST INTO THE ROOM wearing the kind of wide Cheshire-cat grin that usually meant trouble.

"I take it that smile means you have a good reason for being late." Emma adjusted her strapless bra. She stood in front of a full-length mirror in the bra and matching white satin panties with thigh-high lacy stockings and heels. It was a good look for her.

She hadn't worked more than a normal, healthy forty-hour workweek in six months, leaving her time to have a real life, which meant she had a little tan to contrast nicely with the white satin.

She'd been able to see Rafe on a nightly basis.

And oh, baby, how they'd used their time wisely. She sighed in blissful pleasure just thinking about all that they'd done together in the past six months.

But now she had to focus. "I need help getting into the dress..." Emma looked at her beautiful veil hanging off the side of the mirror and had to let out a smile. She couldn't wait to walk down the aisle toward the rest of her life, toward the best thing that had ever happened to her—Rafe.

"They came," Amber said.

"What came?"

Amber hoisted the box she held until she had Emma's full attention. Then, still grinning, she ripped into it and pulled something out.

It looked like—

"No," Emma whispered, but Amber only laughed.

"Yes," she confirmed. "Our fantasy calendars have arrived."

Emma took the calendar from her sister's fingers and opened it up, gaping like a fish out of water at the sight of the tall, leggy brunette wearing nothing more than white filmy material in a lush Hawaiian rain forest. Glowing skin, captivating smile and the eyes…full of so much it took Emma's breath.

She couldn't stop staring. "My God. This is…me."

"Yep."

She flipped to the next page, having to smile at the red halter top and denim shorts that made her look…well, hot. "Wow."

"Look at the rest. It's amazing."

Emma turned the pages and examined each one. By the time she was done, she was grinning. Laughing, she set the calendar aside long enough to step into her wedding dress—with Amber's help. Grabbing up the calendar again, she said, "Let's go. I want to show Rafe."

''Not before the wedding! It's bad luck.''

That had Emma laughing even harder. ''Are you kidding? This calendar is our good luck charm. I bet he's in his dressing room swearing at his tux as he tries to get into it after months and months of never wearing more than a pair of cargo shorts and a T-shirt. Are you coming?''

Amber linked her arm into her sister's. ''And miss out on the chance to see the groom, and hopefully his best man—soon to be my groom—in their skivvies? Let's go, sis.''

And off Emma went, calendar in one hand, her sister in the other, to see her husband-to-be. Off to the rest of her life.